EVERYTHING
leads back to Alice

CHRIS MARRS

EVERYTHING
leads back to Alice...

and Josh,

There's always a
Story!
Best,
Chris Marrs

BAD MOON BOOKS

ANAHEIM - CALIFORNIA

FIRST EDITION

Everything Leads Back to Alice
© 2013 by Chris Marrs

Cover Art © 2013 by GAK

Book Design
by César Puch

Copy Editing
by Steve Souza & Jamie La Chance

Bad Moon Books logo created by Matthew JLD Rice

ISBN-10: 0989744337
ISBN-13: 978-0-9897443-3-1

 BAD MOON BOOKS
1854 W. Chateau Ave.
Anaheim, CA 92804
USA

www.badmoonbooks.com

*For my parents who,
through sharing their love of
reading with their children,
sparked the desire to create
worlds of my own.*

ACKNOWLEDGEMENTS

First I'd like to thank Roy Robbins and Liz Scott for taking the chance on this new writer and her novella. Gene O'Neill and Gord Rollo for providing a first read and for their extremely insightful and helpful comments. Butch and Harry for the support and friendship. Mark Salter for allowing me to pick his brain in regards to his vast knowledge of handguns. Any mistakes are mine. To all my writer and non-writer friends, I'm looking at you Cloud Cutter One, who have inspired me to keep reaching whether they realize it or not. Thank you, all.

No, They Can't Do That

Little girls in school can't do math. Later, college women go into the Humanities, skipping the Sciences. Women don't make good department chairs at universities.

Women don't make good leaders or CEOs of companies. Women aren't able to adapt to combat positions in the military. Women aren't good at jobs that require cool under stress, like airline pilots. And of course, with their sensibilities, women don't make good horror writers. Of course all these stereotypes are inaccurate, perhaps nothing more than a kind of perpetuated bigotry.

In current literature I would suggest that two of the very finest dark fiction writers are Lisa Morton and Roberta Lannes. From my outsider viewpoint I suspect both these excellent writers are of the female persuasion.

I have stated elsewhere that the health of the genre can be best determined by the quality of the emerging young writers. In the past wave of ten years to the present, I'd guess that there have been a number of very good women writers. In the present wave of emerging ten or twelve good writers, I'd suggest the best are all female. Perhaps the one exhibiting the most potential of this group is Chris Marrs.

Chris's strengths: Her prose is always highly polished, the precise word selected, especially the correct verb, which reduces the need for extra adjectives and adverbs. Therefore, she often does *more with less*. Often the reader finds colorful, concrete images embedded in her text. But perhaps her greatest strength is the reality exhibited in her characters' makeup and especially in their complex relationships with other characters. No simple comic book stereotypes in this writer's work. No, and I suspect the complexities detailed in her relationships are probably autobiographical. *Alice* is a good example of the very complex relationships and motivations between a mother-son-girlfriend, an excellent novella, with some truly scary scenes.

So, read *Alice* and two upcoming short stories, *Twisted Sister* and *Paper And Pencil, Skin And Ink*, in an upcoming issue of Dark Discoveries and the eagerly anticipated *A Darke Phantastic*. Then, see if you agree that Chris Marrs is an emerging dark fiction star.

Oh, like her colleagues Lisa and Roberta, Chris doesn't flinch from her firm convictions.

Might not be a good idea to suggest that: *No, women writers can't write horror.*

—Gene O'Neill
Napa, CA 2013

EVERYTHING
leads back to Alice

Mike, Early Spring, Connecticut, Present

Mike sat on a park bench, puke crusted his chin and shirt, and tears streamed down his face. The tang of wood smoke hung in the cool air and dew soaked his socks. His Nissan Xterra sat with one tire atop the curb while the ass end invaded the adjoining parking spot. Mike took a hit from the bottle of Jack Daniel's he held in his hand. Bits and pieces of why he'd arrived on the bench were beginning to come together. Images of Jane throwing him out of their house, his boss telling him not to come back to work, and the glint of light off a bottle took their turn in his thoughts. He stared at the revolver in his other hand.

The gun felt simultaneously light and heavy. Nothing to live for. He put the barrel of the revolver in his mouth, tasted metal—sharp and cold—tasted the slick and bitter oil then removed it to take a swig of bourbon. Then, he put the handgun to his temple.

"Go home, Mike," Alice said from his side. She wore neither coat over her slender frame nor cap, and the streetlight tinted her white-blonde hair with orange and made her blue eyes seem black.

"I can't. Jane kicked me out months ago," he said. "Nothing left. Not even you."

"Go home," she said. "Home to Fallen's Island."

The scent of salt water and seaweed filled his nostrils and the lonely screech of a gull wormed its way into his ears. *Home.*

"Find me, Mike," she said.

He banged the gun down onto the bench and said, "I am trying to. I've spent the last twenty years searching for you."

ℬℭ

Daylight streamed in through the windshield and blazed into Mike's eyelids to burn his eyes. He groaned. His mouth was pasty with a coat of vomit, his stomach was a mess of roiling acid. He shifted in his seat. *Where am I?* Tentatively, he opened his eyes and closed them again to block the glare. He tried once more. This time the light wasn't so harsh and he saw a towering line of maple trees stretch down the street. Stately homes sat on manicured lawns touched by a light frost. His senses awoke and he shivered, his muscles sore from the cold settling in while he'd slept, been passed out. A gun lay on the passenger seat. *What did I do?*

While he tried to puzzle out the murk of the night before, the nausea overcame him sending him to fumble with the door handle. Sweat broke out along his hairline as his stomach lurched and his throat convulsed, then the door popped open. He leaned out and heaved. A thin stream of amber liquid drooled onto the pavement. His stomach spasmed and hurled hot, yellow bile into the mix. When the tempest passed, he wiped his chin and sat up, abdominal muscles quivering from strain.

A group of girls, wearing what he presumed were school uniforms, walked past in that lazy, disjointed fashion preteens had. One girl, pretty in a snobbish way, glanced at him. She wrinkled her nose, pointed him out to her girlfriends who, in turn, wrinkled their noses and laughed. No doubt they'd witnessed his performance. He pictured how he must look to them. A puking man with disheveled hair, bloodshot eyes, and the stubble of yesterdays beard, a drunk basically, couldn't be a pretty sight. Driven by shame, he turned the key and the truck started with a soft roar, then he peeled away while repeating to himself that he wasn't a drunk, he could quit anytime.

It wasn't until he rounded the first corner that he realized he'd been parked in front of Alice's parents' house. Trying to outrun the blank spot in his mind while praying the gun hadn't come into play at some point, he drove through the affluent streets of the Connecticut suburb. Last year he'd followed Alice's parents here in hopes that she'd return to them. Following the familiar route, he guided the truck toward the *Lazy Daffodil Inn*, a run-down forgotten joint once catering to tourists, where he'd been staying since Jane kicked him out.

Mike parked the truck, tucked the gun under his shirt—he wouldn't want someone to find it—then got out to unlock the room door. Inside, the stench of old booze, stale pizza, and dirty laundry fouled the air. The comforter sat in a ball on a worn carpet dotted here and there with cigarette burns and stains he didn't want to identify. The sweat-stained sheets lay twisted on the bed. He turned on a lamp then sat on the bed with the handgun in his hand. When had his life become so low?

He turned the revolver and pushed the latch that released the cylinder. The blunt end of six bullets looked back at him.

He shut it. The handgun had been an ex-girlfriend's. She'd bought it for protection after a rash of burglaries in her apartment complex. While in a rage at her for breaking up with him, he'd stolen it out of her nightstand. He couldn't remember why they broke up, something to do with how she felt she'd never measure up. Didn't matter, anyway, he thought, she'd been only one in a parade of failed romances. He tossed the gun onto the nightstand where it clattered against his cell phone.

The *one missed call* and *new voicemail* icons taunted him from the face of the cell. Fearful of what he might hear, he picked it up and pushed the password that allowed Jane's voice to echo in his head. Apparently, he'd shown up at her house and begged for her back, which caused a scene with the neighbors and the threat of police. Another humiliating moment added to the stack of others that'd been his life since he'd ran away from home, ran away to find Alice. A flash of a park bench, a glimmer of conversation, and then waking up in front of her parents house summed up his night. Somehow, everything always led back to Alice, and Alice led back to home.

He looked around the room. The empty bottles and broken pizza boxes reminded him that he had nothing left. Maybe it was time.

ৎৎ৩

Sue, Early Spring, Fallen's Island, Present
Sue descended the basement steps, the dirt floor making squeaky crunching sounds as she made her way to the other room. A washing machine and dryer sat, quiet, along one wall, a freezer along the opposite, and the opening to the pantry gaped from the wall between. Beside it was the door to her doll

room, the place she stored the most precious of her collection. She drew a little key out of her pocket, used it to open the padlock, and entered the room.

From the shelves that lined the walls, the dolls looked at her. Blue-eyed ones, brown, green, and violet-eyed ones, boys and girls, toddlers and babies, some dressed in costumes depicting other cultures or time periods, others in baby clothes, they were her children, her babies. Their glass eyes seemed to sparkle with enjoyment and contentment. All except the three howling little ones in bassinets that took center stage. Those babies she considered the most cherished, and special, of her collection.

Her heart ached with their cries and she leaned over the bassinets to coo at them. When her soft placations didn't sooth them, she went over and, in turn, rocked each bassinet. Finally, their wailing wound down until all was silent again. Sue sat down in her rocking chair and picked up a book of fairytales, but before she started reading, a multitude of voices whispered loudly, *they're back.*

Their words stole her breath.

ဆဝ ဗ

Mike, Early Spring, Fallen's Island, Present
The little ferry swayed, the motion exacerbating Mike's hangover. His stomach flip-flopped as he broke out in a boozy smelling sweat. *Shouldn't have ripped it up in Seattle last night.* But he'd been celebrating having made it across the country with hardly a drop to drink. Figured he deserved a night out. Besides, he had a bit of money now since, when he'd hit Detroit, he'd traded his Xterra for a Toyota Camry and a couple thousand in cash. The money should, if he was careful, last until he

decided whether he was going to stay or go, whether he'd find what he was looking for or not.

A commercial fish boat, on its way out to sea, chugged by and left a series of waves behind. The ferry dipped and lurched as the surges rolled past. Mike leaned his chin on his chest and pinched the bridge of his nose to ride it out. Once the worst had settled down, he blew out a heavy breath, leaned his head against the headrest, and decided he should have let his mom know he was coming back. But twenty years had slipped away without speaking to her. He didn't know how she'd react to his return. Even after all this time, she may hold a grudge and not have forgiven him for leaving. Hell, he didn't know if seeing her would bring back the old anger in him. Still, though, she was his mom.

He picked his cell phone up off the passenger seat and saw the *no service* icon. Of course there'd be no service out on the ocean, and might not be in town either. The sense of relief the delayed conversation brought didn't shock him. He wasn't quite ready to speak with her, much less have her try to convince him to stay at the house. It dawned on him then he hadn't arranged for a place to stay. The only place he could think of was *Molly May's B&B*. They used to take in boarders during the off-season and he wondered if they still did, granted if they were even around after all these years.

The lackluster grey of the ocean and low hanging clouds created a dreary image to go with his thoughts and a light drizzle started to fall. Through the cracked open window, a breeze carried the scent of rotting seaweed and diesel fuel, and pushed a bead of sweat into his eye. Mike sucked in a quick breath at the sting and in the brief moment while the sweat muddled his vision, he thought he saw Alice standing on the bow. She wore the same clothes she'd been wearing when he first met her.

The ferry's engines changed from a growl to a whine as it neared the terminal, the commercial fishing dock sliding past on the right. A bump, then the metal ramp scraped along concrete while Mike, along with five other passengers on board, started their engines. The ramp attendant gave the all-clear and started directing them off the boat. The car jostled as the surface under the tires changed from metal to concrete and Mike was back on Fallen's Island.

Local history said the island was originally supposed to be called Fallon's Island, after the family who'd owned it, but a mix up with the cartographers forever dubbed it Fallen's. Local gossip also said the family didn't have it corrected as the island was where the troublesome middle son lived. He'd built a mansion on the bluff and called the bay it overlooked, Cyrus' Bay. Sometime in the early 1900s, he'd abandoned the island for Seattle. Rumor had it he'd left his serving staff and their families to fend for themselves in the little village of fishermen and loggers that had sprung up along the shore of the bay. The village grew into a town and became Shelter By the Bay, due to the way its curve protected the town from storms. Simply, Shelter Bay to the locals. The mansion sat empty and rotting until it was bought in the 1990s and converted into *The Crystal Palace Resort*.

He touched the gas and the Toyota, engine straining, shot up the incline. At the crest of the slope, concrete gave way to the pavement road leading toward the town on the opposite side of the island. Mike followed it through a curve, eased off the peddle when his mom's street came up on the right, then, not at all surprised at the dread he felt, punched it.

Cedar trees whipped past, their towering boughs stretching across the road to create a canopy. The shush-shush of the tires on the wet pavement and the infrequent squeak of the wind-shield wipers were the only sounds. With each passing mile, the trees grew closer to the road. Moss blanketed the ground around their trunks, and the shadows deepened. He shivered and turned up the heat as the temperature dropped. The car rounded another corner and the river came into view. It flowed alongside the road then slid under the bridge marking the edge of town. The smooth hum of tires changed to the bumpy grumble of the wooden bridge.

Soon the forest gave way to the first smattering of houses. For every two homes, well-kept and surrounded by groomed lawns, there was one with peeling paint and an abandoned car on blocks or a rusting appliance of some sort on the shaggy, weed choked grass. As the houses grew closer together, the run down ones became fewer and fewer until Mike was passing a gas station, with two pumps and one bay, on one side of the road and a small convenience store on the other.

The road leading to *The Crystal Palace* flashed by on the left. The first four-way stop, the unofficial marker to the start of main street, Fallon's Way, lay up ahead. A post office sat on the right and the Anglican Church on the left. Mike stopped. The windshield wipers double thumped leaving smears of rain in their wake and turned the elderly woman shuffling across the crosswalk into a distorted blob. Once she reached the other side, the sudden need to see if things had changed sent him straight instead of left to the B&B.

Few people, probably locals since the tourist season hadn't yet begun, wandered the sidewalks. As he drove, he noticed not too much had changed. Many of the kitschy stores he remembered from his youth were still there. The tourist trade kept them alive. Nestled among the kitsch shops were *Harold* and *Son's Hardware, Clothing by Carmichael,* the second hand bookstore: *Reread Me,* and, bluntly, *The Pharmacy.* Mike remembered Sid Chute, the owner, to be a to-the-point man who'd made him nervous. Mike was pleased to see *The Do Duck In,* a greasy spoon he'd frequented as a teen, still there. A little farther down, *Wheat'N'Beans* bakery and coffee shop then he was at the end of the main drag.

Turning right would take him to the little hospital, left would eventually loop him back to the four-way stop at the top of the street. If he went straight, he'd be in the parking lot of *Ocean's View Restaurant and Pub,* a place accommodating tourists and only open during the summer. He went left and toward *Molly May's.*

A few easy minutes later, Mike pulled up in front of the Cape Cod-style house, the sign in the front yard announcing it had remained a B&B, and got out. The raucous calls of kids at play and the clink-clink of swings carried from the school yard. Through the sparse line of trees running along the edge of the backyard, Mike saw the dull white boards and windows of the school. Memories crowded forward, each calling out for attention, but he pushed them away. He walked up the cracked sidewalk leading to the door and rang the bell. The door creaked open.

"Can I help you?" said the plump lady who was not Molly. She appeared about Mike's age but he didn't recognize her.

"I was wondering if you rented out your rooms to boarders?" he said.

He lingered while she appraised him, her mouth stretched in a thin line and arms crossed under her considerable breasts. Her gaze ticked to the Toyota, his clothes, the dark blonde stubble of his unshaven face, then shook her head.

"Nope. Sorry," she said and started to close the door but a shout from the interior halted her.

"Mike Connors?" a male voice said. A thin, reedy man, his receding dark hair peppered with grey, took hold of the door, and opened it all the way. Mike tried to place him. "It's okay, Sylvia, I know him. He's alright."

Sylvia huffed and said, "Fine then. He can have a room by the week. Cash upfront. Once the tourists start rolling in, he'll have to go."

"Sound good to you, Mike?" the man said.

"Uh, yeah, sure. Thanks," he said.

"You don't remember me do you?"

Mike wracked his brain trying to come up with a name but failed so he gave the man a sheepish grin.

"No, I'm sorry, I don't," Mike said.

"Doug. Doug Williams," Doug said. His brown eyes seemed to beg Mike to remember him.

Mike's grin turned into a smile of recognition and he said, "Of course. You've changed."

"Haven't we all. Well, maybe not you so much. You look almost the same as you did in school."

Mike had nothing to say to that. If he correctly recalled, he and Doug weren't exactly the best of friends back then.

Doug clapped his hands together and said, "Okay then. Well, bring your bags in and we'll get you settled."

Once Mike had brought in his bag and they'd situated him in one of the rooms overlooking the school, *good times, huh, Mike,* he wandered down to the kitchen. Sylvia puttered around the stove, dropping carrots into a soup pot, then stirring its contents. The smell of baking bread made his mouth water. Doug bounced in.

"So, what brings you back?" Doug said as he sat on one of the stools sitting around the butcher block. He pulled another out and indicated Mike should take a seat, too.

"Needed a change, I guess," Mike said as he sat. "Hey, what happened to Molly?"

"She moved to Florida, claimed the sun would do her arthritic bones a world of good," Doug said. "So, she sold the place to my lovely wife and I."

"Not so much sold as gave," Sylvia said. "She's my aunt."

Mike looked closer at Sylvia and saw the coltish girl with the doe-like green eyes who'd occasionally spent her summers here. Their eyes met and she blushed as she went back to stirring the soup. Vaguely, he remembered spending part of one summer with her until someone new came along to snag his attention. Mike cleared his throat.

"I have to ask," Doug said. "Did you and Sylvia ever…you know?"

Mike almost fell off the stool. Sylvia slammed the wooden spoon down on the stove.

"Douglas Williams, what a thing to ask," she said with disgust and embarrassment.

Mike didn't want to get caught in the middle of this so he stood and said, "You know. I've had a long day. Think I'll go up to my room for a while. Probably won't see me until morning."

"I'm sorry, was that the wrong thing to say?" Doug said.

The combination of utter innocence on Doug's face, and hangover made Mike cranky. He almost wanted to punch Doug but he held it in check, Doug was only trying to be sociable, however awkward he was at it.

"No worries. I'm just tired," Mike said. "Have a good night."

Mike left the warm comfort of the kitchen, tense murmurs following him to the bedroom. In the room, his bag lay on the floral comforter covering the bed so he moved it to the floor. It clinked. He knew what made the sound and wondered what possessed him to stash a bottle of Jack inside. Coming here was supposed to be an escape from the troubles that'd plagued him. But, since he felt the Jack shouldn't go to waste, he took it out and broke the seal. A little hair of the dog to quell the hangover and help him slide into sleep seemed like a good idea. He'd quit tomorrow.

The bourbon slid down his throat, calmed his acidic stomach, and smoothed the rough edge of his headache. Enjoying the relief it brought, he did it again. And again and one more wouldn't hurt. A warm glow settled over him.

Mike went to the window, the bottom half opaque with condensation, and stared out into the darkening night at the shadowy form of the school. His gaze traveled over the playground then over to the annex that housed the high school rooms. Good times, Doug had said. And Mike agreed. Him and his friends had ruled the school back then. He wondered, as he turned away from the window, what had happened to them. However, a reflection in the glass gave him pause. Alice.

Her hand came up and she traced a heart into the condensation but the beads of water remained unbroken.

"Remember the beginning?" Alice said from beside him. "I do."

And wasn't this why Alice had led him home, to relive their short time together so Mike could finally let her go. All the choices Mike had made during the last twenty years led here, led to Alice.

ౚ ⋙

Mike, Early Spring, Senior Year, 1992

Mike tossed his books into his locker then slammed it shut. The catcalls, laughter, and general chatter filling the crowded hallway drowned the sound out. He turned and sprinted through the teenagers milling about. Mr. Hamilton would be pissed if Mike was late for work again. Probably make him scrape the barnacles off the bottom of the boat or something else just as horrible. Doug, a loser in a plaid flannel shirt and Doc Martens, suddenly stepped out of a classroom. Mike shifted his weight in order to avoid Doug but was too slow. They landed together on the floor in a tangle of legs and arms.

"Get off me, you fag," Mike said as he rolled the scrawny, stupid idiot off him.

Doug tumbled into the bank of lockers and said, "Asshole."

Everyone stopped what they were doing, the atmosphere taking on a palpable tension. In the hush, Mike stood up and some jerkoff yelled "Fight, fight!" but Mike wouldn't waste his time on a fight. Wasn't worth it. Slower now, he strode from the scene. Chatter filled the vacuum as everyone resumed putting books away, filling backpacks with homework, or standing around talking.

Mike, his mind once again on getting down to the docks, neared the door and saw a vision of beauty coming through it. Flanked by a well-dressed couple, she sauntered down the hallway toward him. The front of his jeans tightened as he watched the way her breasts bounced with each hip-swinging step.

Her blonde hair shimmered under the fluorescent light. Amusement danced in her blue eyes as if she'd witnessed the little drama and found it funny. When she passed him, the mingled scents of vanilla and musk and green apples made him think those were the best things he'd ever smelled. And he wondered who she was. He wouldn't find out until lunch the next day.

ಬಿ ೮೪

Mike sat on the hallway floor, his back against the lockers, with Tanya, Adrienne, Jay, and Andrew. The other high school kids milled around or sat in groups while the elementary kids squealed and laughed outside. Odors of salami and apples killed the scent of sneakers left in lockers. Tanya stroked his leg and asked him a question but he didn't notice. The apple scent reminded him of the mystery girl and he speculated why she hadn't been at school this morning.

"Yo, Mike," Jay said.

Jay's voice dragged Mike back to reality, "What?"

"You coming to the bonfire tomorrow night or not?" Jay said.

"I'd like it if you came," Tanya said and squeezed his thigh.

He batted her hand away. She glared at him and, under her breath, called him a douche. Like he cared.

"Sure, my boss has to go to the mainland tomorrow so I have the day off," he said.

"Awesome," Andrew said. "My brother said he'd score us some beer. Good times."

Then there *she* was in a styling shirt and faded jeans, cuffs rolled just the right way at the ankle, walking over to them. She wormed her way between Mike and Tanya and the warmth of her shoulder pressed against his did funny things to his mind.

"I'm Alice," she said as Tanya shot a killing scowl at the back of her head then rolled her eyes at Adrienne. Jay and Andrew stared in appreciation. "And you're…"

Mike's tongue stuck to the roof of his mouth.

"I'm Jay, this is Andrew, and the idiot who can't talk is Mike," Jay said.

Adrienne punched Jay on the shoulder, "And what are we? Chopped liver?"

"Gear down," Jay said and rubbed his shoulder. "These bitches are Adrienne and Tanya."

"Fuck off, Jay," Tanya said. To Alice she said, "Ignore him, he only thinks he's funny."

Mike listened to all this with detachment. *Alice, her name is Alice.*

"Mike. I'm Mike," he blurted out. God, he sounded like such a loser. He wished the floor would open up and swallow him.

"Nice to meet you, Mike," Alice said. She smiled at him and he ceased wanting to disappear. "So, what do you all do for fun around here?"

"There's a bonfire tomorrow night. You can come if you want," Andrew said. Tanya scowled at him, he turned to her and said, "What?" Her scowl deepened.

As if sensing trouble, Alice said, "Oh, a bonfire? How rustic. Where?" Mike wasn't sure if she mocked them or not, but, as long as she wanted to go, he didn't care.

Andrew started to answer but Mike cut him off, "Over by the dock on the other side of the island. No one will bother us there."

"That's if Mike's mom doesn't pull out her binoculars to spy on her little boy and ruin our fun by calling the cops," Jay said.

Again, being swallowed by the floor appealed to Mike.

"Shut up, fag," Mike said. "At least it won't be my dad showing up to bust the party."

"At least my dad is still around."

"Boys, boys," Alice said. She flashed Mike another smile. One that said, to him, boys fighting in her presence wasn't new to her. "You settle down now."

"Where are you from?" Tanya said. Mike took it to be an attempt to divert the conversation.

"Everywhere." Alice said. "My dad's a Master Chef so we move around a lot. He's here to open the restaurant at *The Crystal Palace*."

"Cool," Adrienne said. She leaned forward to look past Tanya—who shot Adrienne one of her dirty looks—at Alice. "My mom's going to be baking up there once they open. She's excited. Says it's fancier than anything she's ever seen."

Mike waited expectantly for Alice's answer but the bell to signal the end of lunch rang, and the reply never came.

⁖⁕

The bonfire was a speck of orange growing larger with every step Mike took. Sand and shells crunched under his feet as his large, angry strides ate up the distance. The crash of drums and driving guitars drowned out the slap of water against the hulls of the boats moored at the dock. Laughter floated his way. Sounded like the party was *happening* and he'd missed most of it. No thanks to his mom. He knew she wouldn't let him go so he had sat, anxious and wanting to see Alice again, until he was certain his mom was asleep. Then he'd snuck down the stairs and out the door.

Sparks spun off into the night to join the stars above. Silhouettes crossed in front of the blaze and he wondered if Alice was one of them. A moan came from his right and he wordlessly cheered the amorous couple on. With luck, it'd be him tonight. Then a lust-filled whisper of a name carried his way, *Alice.*

Mike stopped, his gut plummeted into his suddenly cold bowels. No. Damn it, he was too late. If only his mom had gone to bed earlier. He shifted his weight from foot to foot. Should he go home or keep going? He really couldn't see the point of joining the party when the reason he'd risked his mom's wrath was hooking up with someone else.

Full throated laughter escaped the confines of the fire's light and he recognized it as Tanya's. Maybe the night wouldn't be a bust after all. Mike stepped forward, a shell snapped under his heel, and the whispers and moans quieted.

"Who's there?" Alice said.

"Just me. I'm only passing through," he said. It sounded resentful.

"Mike is that you?" she said.

"Yeah, but don't let me stop you. Carry on."

"Help me," Alice said.

Confused, Mike paused and scanned the dark for her. *What did she mean, help her?*

"What the hell are you playing at, Alice," Jay said. Mike's heart dropped farther.

"Jay's outta control," Alice said.

"Fuck you, I am. You started it," Jay said.

"What part of 'no' don't you understand?" she said.

That did it. The hair on the back of his neck and the veins in his forearms throbbed when he fisted his hands. The bastard. He ran to where he thought they were. In the beam of a flashlight set on the sand, he saw Alice, her shirt open, trying to push Jay off her. Mike grabbed Jay by his collar and hauled him back. He let go. Jay stumbled and landed on his rear, a bewildered look on his face. Alice jumped up and wrapped Mike in her embrace. He felt her trembling.

"Oh, sure, act all innocent now, you crazy-ass bitch," Jay said.

"Get lost, Jay, before I beat the shit out of you," Mike said as he put an arm around Alice. Part of him soared when she snuggled in closer.

Jay got up, brushed the sand from his pants, and took a step toward them. Mike pushed Alice behind him, and, with shoulders back, spine straight, and chin out, tried to use his size and extra couple inches to intimidate Jay.

"I gotcha," Jay said and backed off.

They watched Jay walk back to the fire, presumably to tell his side of the story before they could ruin his reputation. The adrenaline whooshed out of Mike's system, and he sagged. Alice's arms snaked around his torso and he turned so he faced her. He looked down and when he saw her smile made a dimple in her cheek, he kissed her. He wasn't able to help himself.

ॐ

Mike, Early Spring, Present

Over the next couple of days, Mike tried to occupy himself by helping Doug repair the fence dividing his yard from the school's. Didn't help. Doug's incessant questions regarding what Mike had been up to for the last twenty years, constant chatter, and need for approval started to get on Mike's nerves. He would sneak into his room for a nip just to deal with Doug. Even though the whiskey took the edge off, Mike felt like he was letting himself down.

Then Sylvia jumped into the mix and nagged him on the reasons why he should be staying with his mom or, at least, to call her, surely she knew he was here by now. Also, his mom wasn't far way, like her aunt in Florida, shouldn't they be together. And he started contemplating finding other accommodations but he needed another bottle of Jack first to quiet his jittering nerves and loosen his mind.

Sweating despite the cool drizzle falling, Mike strode across the parking lot and into Eugene's Market. The sudden change in temperature dried the sweat under his arms and made him shiver. A till bleeped and the wheel of a cart squealed. The odor of musty oranges, paper bags, and an undercurrent of cleaner assailed him as he navigated the produce area.

Shoppers flicked past his periphery. A little girl went screaming past him into the aisle, followed close behind by a boy, and Mike jumped back to avoid knocking them over. He turned to snarl at them to be careful when he saw a woman walking toward him. Her blue eyes ticked across his face like she knew him then met his gaze and held it. Blonde hair fell across her narrow shoulders. She smiled and raised a hand in a wave and time stopped.

He felt like a slack-jawed jackass staring at her. *She was here all this time?* All those years he'd followed her parents from city to city, town to town, hoping she'd return to them, and she'd been here all along. He didn't know whether to laugh, cry, or yell.

"Oh my god, Mike, I can't believe it's you," she said.

Within the voice made husky by age, he heard the girl she'd once been and knew it wasn't Alice. His shoulders relaxed and his knees stopped threatening to give out.

"You're looking good, Tanya. When did you decide to go blonde?" he said and put his trembling hands in his pockets.

"Twenty years go by without speaking and that's what you ask me?" she said and laughed. Crow's feet crinkled the corners of eyes underscored with dark circles. "No, 'how are you, how's life been treating you?'"

"Okay, I'll play. How are you? How's life been treating you?"

"Pretty good, actually. And you?"

Falling back into the easy rapport they'd always shared, he said, "That's it? Pretty good? No, 'I went and got married and have twelve kids?'"

A shadow crossed her face but then she smiled and said, "Never married. No kids, either. I've been too busy chasing dreams."

That makes two of us.

"I'd love to stay and catch up but I've gotta run," she said. "What are you doing later? Care to join me for happy hour at *The Dirty Birdie*?"

The Dirty Birdie was the nickname for *The Heron's Roost* pub, a joint frequented largely by the locals. It had earned it's name in a time when commercial fishing and logging were the island's main form of commerce instead of tourism. Any given night of the week the pub would have been packed with the loud, rowdy fishermen and loggers, and barely a night passed without a fist fight. In an effort to entertain his clientele, and keep them from tearing the place apart, the owner brought in a blues singer from the mainland. He had good intentions in mind and Birdie entertained all right. Only most of it was done out back and the nickname was born.

"Sure, if you don't mind being seen with an out of shape middle aged man who used to be somebody," he said.

"As long as you have no objections to escorting a washed up actress," she said. "How does three sound?"

"Sounds like a plan. Looking forward to it."

"Me, too." And when she went by him, she ran a hand along his lower back then continued to the cashier.

He watched the way her hips swayed and hair bounced along her back and felt the tell-tale tingle in his groin. She definitely looked better as a blonde. This might turn out to be an interesting day. He tore his gaze away then proceeded to the back of the store where rows of wine and spirits pointed the way to the coolers of beer. He snagged a bottle of Jack, then, almost like an after thought, grabbed another.

ଧⓒଷ

Mike sat on his bed, sipping the Jack and reading a book about Fallen's Island he'd found on the bookshelf in the common room to kill time before meeting Tanya. A knock on the door startled him.

"Come in. I'm decent," he said as he laid the book facedown and open to keep his page.

Doug poked his head in, noticed the Jack, then sighed. Furtively, he sidled into the room, closing the door behind him.

"We have to talk," Doug said. His eyes darted about the room and refused to settle on Mike.

"Go ahead," Mike said.

"It's your drinking, Mike," Doug said. "Sylvia doesn't like it."

The unfairness of Doug's words made the vein in Mike's temple throb and bounce.

"That's her problem, isn't it?" Mike said.

"No, Mike, it's your problem." Doug shuffled his feet. "She doesn't want a drinker staying here."

"I'm not a drunk, Doug." His tongue suddenly yearned for the smooth liquor so close at hand, yet so distant.

"I don't know where you've been or what you've done since you left but I know the signs of an alcoholic when I see them." Finally, he looked at Mike and offered him a weak shrug. "I don't want you to go. Honestly, we need your money and you've been a big help with the fence so, just slow down on the sauce. All right? Trust me when I say you don't want to be having this conversation later on with Sylvia."

"Duly noted." Mike picked his book up. "Now if you don't mind."

The door snicked shut and Mike lowered the book. Damn it, he wasn't a drunk and if those two didn't badger him with their curiosity and opinions on what he should be doing, he wouldn't drink. He was already planning on finding other accommodations and they'd given him the perfect excuse to do so without hurt feelings.

~ ~ ~

Sue, Early Spring, Present
Sue stormed out of *The Crystal Palace*, her mood matched the grey clouds gathering on the horizon like a promise of violence. Her hands ached from folding the enormous amount of laundry needed in order to have the resort ready for the upcoming season. The chilly bite in the wind seeped between the teeth of her coat zipper and she shivered. Those discomforts were nothing but an annoyance compared to learning secondhand Michael was on the island. *How dare he not even bother to call.* Although she didn't condone it, she could understand why he hadn't shown up at home yet. Michael always avoided

conflict when it suited him best. If, when, he did grace her with his presence she would try not to show her hurt. Oh, how she wanted to track him down and give him a piece of her mind, though. But she wouldn't. She knew if she did, it might drive him away for good.

She brought her car keys out of the purse slung on her shoulder and unlocked the door, a habit gained a couple summers ago by a spate of thefts. Although the culprit had been caught, and the rest of the town went back to the old way of not locking their doors, she never did. Sue tossed her purse on the passenger's seat, then sat in the driver's and started the car.

The fan blasted cold air into her face while fog crept up the windshield. She waited for the fan to blow hot and dispel the vapor. While waiting, she drummed her fingers on the steering wheel in time with Patsy Cline's *Just Out of Reach* playing on the radio and wondered what brought Michael back. The haze crawled farther up the window before it stopped and started to recede. She fumbled behind her for her seatbelt. The strap clicked twice and stopped, she yanked on it but it stayed fast. Sue turned to see what it'd hung up on and a bone-numbing cold enveloped her. It carried weight and felt as if someone were leaning over her from the passenger seat. Feeling like a fool, she peeked over her right shoulder. No surprise the seat was empty. She refocused on her seatbelt and jerked back.

Two words and a symbol stood out against the vapor on the driver's side window:

I'm back ♡

She swore they weren't there a minute ago. Then the cold was gone, not slowly dissipating as the fan emitted hot air but completely vanished. Tires squealed on the pavement as she reversed and tore out of the parking lot. Michael coming back was forgotten as an inexplicable desire to return home to her children overcame her.

‽℄

Mike, Early Spring, Present

At five to three, Mike pulled into the near empty parking lot of *The Dirty Birdie*. The pub was situated far from the main drag and stood among towering cedars whose boughs reached out as if to protect the drinkers inside. In the two large plate glass windows, the reflection of the lot and street behind him concealed whomever might be sitting inside. A bush-beaten Ford F-150 and a classic Honda Civic were the only vehicles. Weird to think that a car from the 1980s was now a classic. The Honda might belong to Tanya, Mike couldn't imagine her in the truck, though she might not be here yet.

Drizzle had become rain and plinked on Mike's head as he crossed the lot. His boots clocked on the sidewalk, echoing in the silence, and the heavy wooden door groaned when he opened it. From the jukebox in the corner, the sounds of Nirvana's *Smells Like Teen Spirit* wafted out into the old fish, old grease, and stale beer redolent air. A drum kit and mikes sat on the little stage at the end of the parquet dance floor, the spot lights dimmed. At the bar running along the left wall, a skinny grizzled man sat with his hunting cap on the bar beside him and a beer mug in his huge hands. Mike thought he recognized him as Mr. Hamilton. If so, the stocky, demanding captain hadn't aged well.

The wing doors separating the kitchen from the rest of the room opened. The bartender, his back turned while he called out a directive to the cook, stepped through. He turned around and Mike felt a rush of familiarity. Even though the man's long hair pulled back in a ponytail had gone white, his broad shoulders showed no signs of a stoop, nor his belly of a paunch.

"John," Mike said. "Can't believe you're still running the place. You're what, close to one hundred now?"

"Mikey!" he said. Mischief crinkled the lines on his face and touched his brown eyes. "You have real ID this time, smartass?"

"I can't believe you remember that," Mike said.

John set down the bottles he carried and waved a dismissive hand, "It's a bartender's job to remember, isn't it? Find a perch at the bar and I'll tap you one."

"Would love to but I'm meeting Tanya."

At the mention of her name, she walked in the door, rounded one of the tables, and wrapped her arms around him in a hug. Taken unaware, he hugged her back. She smelled of vanilla, green apples and sugary liquor. *Where's the musk?* He shook his head to rid the random thought. This was Tanya, not Alice.

Breaking the embrace, she looked up at him and said, "That's your welcome back hug but I should be punching you for leaving in the first place."

"Glad you chose the hug," he said.

"Me, too," she said.

"The usual, Tanya?" John asked.

"You know it," she said. "What're you drinking, Mike? It's on me today."

"Shot of Jack with a beer chaser, John. Mug of whatever you have on tap's fine, thanks."

John poured the shot, drew the draught, and started Tanya's *usual*, involving ice, a metal shaker, and too many ingredients for Mike to consider replicating.

"How's the hunt going, Tanya?" John said, the cubes rattling around the inside of the container as he shook it up and down.

Tanya laughed at the apparent inside joke and said, "No need to revoke my hunting license yet. Might have bagged me a big one."

John poured the pink colored concoction into a chilled martini glass, added a lime wedge, then slid all three drinks across the bar.

"Well then, you kids have fun," he said and winked at Mike.

"Thanks for buying," Mike said when they'd sat at a booth by one of the windows.

"No prob. Consider it your welcome back party," she said.

"First a hug and now a party, huh. You're going to spoil me."

"And is there anything wrong with that?" She gave him a half-smile then raised her glass. "To Mike's return to Fallen's Island."

"And, to the Class of '92." He hadn't planned on saying that, and judging by the way Tanya grimaced then quickly composed herself, she hadn't expected him to either.

They clinked glasses. Mike slammed back the shot and chased the heat with icy beer. Tanya sipped her martini while watching him over the rim of the glass. She set it down then reached over and traced circles on the back of his hand. Her fingers felt cool on his warm skin.

"I just realized something. Now that you're back, the gang's all here," she said.

No, there was still one of them missing, but didn't voice his thought.

If Tanya knew the reason for his silence, she pretended otherwise and said, "You and I were the only ones who left. The rest, well, they stayed and grew up." A wistful expression skipped across her features, here then gone. "So, tell me, what did you grow up to be?" Then held up her hand to stop him from answering. "Wait, let me guess. A lawyer like you planned? You were certainly smart enough. Popular and smart, a force to be reckoned with back then."

"Nope. I ended up floating around from place to place, job to job, and landed in real estate but I wasn't very good at it. When the economy tanked, I was one of the first my boss let go," he said. She stopped drawing invisible circles on his hand and took another drink. "Sorry to disappoint."

"No, not disappointed. Okay, a little bit. You had so much potential but you threw it all away."

Choosing not to deal with her statement, he finished his beer before asking, "And what about you? What did you grow up to be?"

"A server for John." She flicked her hair out of her eyes and Mike read bitterness in the motion. "I couldn't make it in L.A. so, when I aged out, I came back here and I work for him Thursday, Friday, and Saturday nights and in the lounge at the resort during the summer."

"Ah, and here I thought you were being cute with the failed actress bit."

"I only wish."

Awkward silence spun between them while the jukebox shuffled and started to play Shinedown's *Her Name is Alice*. John slipped in and replaced their empty glasses with full ones. The distraction broke the discomfort and, after a minute of stilted conversation, they resumed catching up. Easy chatter and light flirtations had them laughing then touching and time flowed seamlessly past.

"Wanna get out of here?" she asked.

"And do what?" he replied.

She didn't answer, just gave his thigh a playful squeeze before sauntering up to the bar to pay the tab. Mike grinned into his mug, and thought, *why not*, Jane was the last women he'd been with. He swilled the rest of his beer then followed Tanya out the door.

ಶಂ ಿ

The counter rammed into his lower back and a martini glass tumbled into the sink full of dirty dishes. He put a hand back to brace himself against her enthusiastic embrace then nibbled at her bottom lip. A moan escaped her throat. His cock responded. He ran a hand along the side of her breast hoping to hear her moan again. She reached a hand down to massage him through his jeans. The barrier between his thumb and her hardened nipple excited and frustrated him. He nuzzled her neck, her blonde hair falling like flax around him, and he breathed in her aromas of vanilla and green apples, of her sex.

"Alice," he murmured.

Tanya's soft, supple body stiffened and her head wrenched back.

ಶಂ ಿ

Sue, Early Spring, Present
Sue sat in the living room, a small cache of her doll collection resting on the shelves behind her, the others safe in their

room downstairs. After reading the disturbing message on the car window, she'd made sure all was well.

The flickering light from the muted TV cast moving shadows around the room as the wind whipped the trees into a fury. Rain pelted against the window. Condensation misted the lower half of the single paned window, as it always did when the house was warm and a storm blew in. Headlights turned the fog opaque. She looked up, hoping it was Michael and half expecting to see writing on the glass, but the car passed without turning in and there weren't any messages for her.

Turning a teacup around in her hands, she noticed how wrinkled they'd become. Funny how your mortality caught up to you at the oddest moments. Her hands reminded her she wasn't young anymore and made her feel like the last rose of summer. In one lifetime, these hands once helped ease infants into this world and, in another, scrubbed toilets and changed linens for the little inn then the resort. The change in occupation was due to a new hospital replacing the outdated clinic. Once it'd been built, using a mid-wife fell out of vogue.

Under the raging of the storm, she heard the gentle tick-tock of the grandfather clock. Tonight the ticks and tocks sounded more mocking than comforting. *Michael's not home,* they seemed to say, *you're all alone.* At least Michael was trying to come home or so she told herself. Broken and saddled with an addiction, if the rumors were true, but he was on the island. Sue put the teacup on the coffee table, her thoughts feeling as if they'd curdled in her head like milk that'd sat out too long. She didn't want to think about Michael.

A chorus of *mama* rang through the room and pulled Sue from her thoughts. She shook her head to clear it of the negative track it was on. Really, she wasn't truly alone, she had her children to take care of. How could she have forgotten it was time for reading them their fairytales?

She refreshed her tea and descended the steps leading to the basement, to her children. Halfway down, she heard their glee.

ঙ০ ৪৩

Mike, Early Spring, Present

"Fucking asshole," Tanya said and pushed him away.

Mike's penis withered. So, he'd messed up and called her Alice, big deal. She needn't have reacted like that, though. Then he noticed she was rubbing the back of her head.

"That hurt," she said. "I'm not against the rough stuff but you gotta warn a girl if you're going to pull her hair like that."

"What? I didn't pull your hair," he said.

"No, then who did?"

As he searched for the answer, the wind buffeted the small trailer making it shake in its vicious onslaught. It whistled past the window and a rush of cold air twisted through the kitchen. The little hairs on Mike's arms stood up. He looked at Tanya, her eyes wide. Blonde hair shimmered in the dark hallway on his right but vanished when he turned to look. *Alice.* But the energy didn't feel like his Alice. It felt like something else, something sinister, then the moment receded. Warmth returned and with it, Mike told himself it was only the storm.

"What the hell was that?" Tanya said. She rubbed her arms and a shiver rolled over her.

He repeated to her what he'd been telling himself. She raised an eyebrow and opened her mouth to presumably contradict him then closed it.

"I need a drink." She pulled the martini glass out of the sink, rinsed it, and starting mixing one of her pink martinis. "You want one?"

The sugary concoction didn't appeal to him, but when in Rome...

"Sure," he said.

She must have heard the hesitation in his voice because she opened a cupboard by the door, moved some bottles around, and said, "Ah-ha." And pulled out a bottle of Wild Turkey. "It's not Jack but how about this instead?"

"Works for me."

Drinks in hand, they moved into a living room reeking of cat piss. A lamp, looking like it'd been rescued from a garage sale sometime during the 1980s, shed weak light. Sheets covered the furniture, probably hiding stains, a small TV sat on a milk crate, and two more served as a coffee table. The only insight into the woman who lived here were the framed theater announcements hanging on the wall. While Tanya went back into the kitchen, he read each one and noticed Tanya's name listed as part of the cast but never the female lead.

"What are you doing here with this bitch?" Alice said. "Go home."

Mike continued to read while he whispered, "Why do you have to do this every time I get a girl?"

"Because they're not me."

Tanya came back, set a pitcher full of pink drink and the bottle of Wild Turkey on the coffee table, and flopped down on the couch. Alice sat on the arm. Mike tried to ignore her.

"So we don't have to get up," Tanya said and patted the couch beside her. "Come sit."

Alice stuck her fingers down her throat like she wanted to puke. He sat. Alice glared at him and disappeared.

They spent the better part of the night drinking and catching up. Tanya regaled him with tales from her days in L.A., he suspected she skipped the bad parts, and he shared his misadventures. Omitting, of course, the part about searching for Alice. When the night wore toward dawn, she asked him to stay. Didn't want to be alone, she'd said. And because he didn't either, he stayed.

ಐಲ

Mike fell out of bed. His sleep-addled brain panicked and forced him to his feet. Who did that? Where was he? The room sharpened into focus. A trail of clothing led from the hallway to the bed and women's clothing, more than one would possibly wear in a day, lay in clumps on the brown carpet. Vanilla permeated the air, the scent of coffee an undertone, and dim light filtered through the sheers. Adrenaline abating, the sourness in his stomach and ache behind his eyes spoke up and reminded him of last night's escapade. He gathered his clothes and put them on then wandered down the hallway. The aroma of coffee grew stronger with each step.

"Good morning, sleepy head," Tanya said from her seat at the table. Her voice sounded cheerful but the bags under her eyes and the way she squinted told him she was hurting. "Help yourself to the coffee."

The carafe chattered against the lip of the mug as he poured.

"What are your plans today?" Tanya said.

Mike picked up the mug and leaned against the counter before he replied, "Probably head back to *Molly May's* and help

Doug finish the fence." She raised her eyebrows in what he took to be surprise. "Why?"

"No reason." It seemed like she wanted to say more but leaned over to stoke the grey tabby winding around her ankles instead. Then she sat back up, a look of sudden determination on her face. "I thought you'd be staying at your mom's. Why don't you come stay here? Doug and Sylvia are such prisses and, besides, I was going to look for a roommate to help with the rent. You can have the spare bedroom, if you want, or…"

His instinct told him he'd regret moving in so soon, but he intended to leave *Molly May's* and her offer lent him an out. Sure, he could stay in her spare bedroom but her unspoken insinuation gave him an idea of what she really wanted. And would that really be so wrong? Part of him, though, chimed up and asked *What about Alice, wouldn't you be betraying her?* But he'd returned to the island to put the past behind him and this would be as good a start as any.

"Are you sure?" he said.

"I'm sure." And he heard in her voice, she was.

"Alright then, roomie, I'll go settle up with Doug and get my bag."

The cat arched its back and hissed, seemingly at nothing, then clawed Tanya on her exposed ankle. She pulled her foot back as the cat shot down the hallway, pausing to hiss once more before disappearing into Tanya's bedroom.

"Fucking Haywire," she said, rubbing her ankle. Her hand came away bloody. "She's never freaked out like that. I hope it doesn't mean she is letting me know she isn't happy with you moving in."

But Mike didn't hear her, the scents of vanilla and musk and green apples distracted him.

⁊✲☙

Mike pulled up in front of his mom's house but didn't get out. Living with Tanya was a blast but the days of vegging on the couch and drinking while she was at work were hard on his bank account, especially since he now shared half of her bills. When he'd left the trailer his intention had been to go down to the dock and scope out the work situation. Instead of going straight, he automatically turned onto his mom's road. By now, she must know he'd come back and Mike worried he'd waited too long before coming to see her. Gathering his courage, and wishing for a drink, he got out of the car and hip checked the door shut.

He took a deep breath of the salty air and turned to face the house with its fading whitewashed boards and black shutters hanging askew. A tentative puff of breeze tousled his hair and rattled the rose bush growing along the front porch. Memories, both light and dark, stirred. He climbed the three steps to the porch while jingling the car keys in his hand.

She'd painted the front door green, and for some reason it bothered him. She'd changed the welcome mat, too. That didn't bother him as much. Mats wore out. He knocked on the door. Stupid really, he should feel like he could walk in but it'd been too long for that. When she didn't answer, he knocked again. Harder. The hollow boom reverberated through the covered porch and startled a sparrow nesting on one of the beams. Mike ducked as it circled his head a couple of times, chirped at him, then took off over the scrub grass and sea peas across the road. He tracked its progress as it flew out over the ocean. His knock remained unanswered.

Her car wasn't in the drive but it didn't mean she wasn't home. It might mean she'd taken to parking it in the detached garage at some point over the years. He tried the knob, locked, so he lifted the new welcome mat and looked for the key she kept under it. There it lay along with the grit and a piece of dried flower. He picked up the key and unlocked the door. *Welcome home*, he thought.

Wild flower sachet mingled with the soft scent of baby powder and pungent garlic to envelop him as he stepped into the foyer. Out of habit, he tossed his keys into the decorative bowl sitting atop a little table. They rattled against the other keys and sounded louder than usual in the stillness. The house had the hollow atmosphere of one that'd been closed up for sometime. From the dining room came the ticking of the grandfather clock, also too loud. Maybe she was away on vacation but she never went anywhere. His eyes fell upon a badly patched hole in the wall between the door and the window. A remnant from his abrupt departure.

"Mom! You home?" Mike called, his eyes still on the patch.

Only the clock answered with its steady tick-tock. He went to the staircase that led up to the bedrooms and bathroom and called again. No reply. Onto the living room where, in the mellowing afternoon light, he saw she'd changed little. The same sofa and armchair, threadbare now, dominated the center, high shelves displaying a part of her doll collection ran the length of one wall, and a TV, the only upgrade, hung on the wall opposite, but no Mom.

He crossed the foyer and a right led him into the dining room. Another empty space, save for the ticking grandfather clock and maple table with matching sideboard. Back to the foyer, then another right took him into the kitchen. Here, too he was met with an unchanged room, right down to the

Formica topped kitchen table and rust-pitted appliances from his youth, but devoid of anything living. The door leading to the basement hung ajar. He pushed it open with his fingertips. Cool air carrying the earthy scent of dirt floors and laundry soap crept into the kitchen and the part of his mind that was still a boy warned him to watch out for monsters.

"Mom? It's Mike," he said.

He leaned forward to peer down the steps and into the dimly lit basement. At the bottom lay a body shaped bundle. The steps shuddered under his weight as he bolted down them, his breath coming out in gasps and the little hairs on the back of his neck stirring. Speed carried him over the figure, he skidded as he turned on his heel then knelt next to a duvet. He stood up, not knowing if he was angry with his mom or himself for thinking it was her, and kicked the blanket. It tangled around his foot, almost tripping him. He cursed as he seized it and dragged the duvet into the laundry room.

The moist, slightly irony odor of the room greeted him when he entered. To the child in him, it smelled of nightmares. He didn't bother to call out for his mom, it was apparent she wasn't here either. So, he tossed the duvet on the washing machine and started to leave but stopped short. Beside the white door of the pantry stood a green door locked by a padlock, rusty from age. The padlock was closed.

The coolness of the basement turned frosty. A feathery touch danced along the back of his neck, goosebumps prickled in its wake. The air in front of him blurred, slivers of blue and blonde gleamed from its center. He heard a giggle.

"Alice?" he said, his voice wobbly.

Before he could ask again, the giggling stopped, and the shimmer disappeared leaving behind the impression of a less loving Alice than the one he spoke to. He wondered if she were punishing him for moving in with Tanya.

Then he realized why his mom painting the front door green bothered him.

ಐ ೞ

Mike, Mid Spring, Senior Year, 1992

"She's not home, is she?" Alice asked in a hushed tone as Mike let her into the house. Her presence lightened the dreary atmosphere.

"No. At work until 5-ish," he said.

Alice visibly relaxed.

"She doesn't like me," she said as Mike took her coat and hung it on the newel post. Drops of rainwater pattered onto the floor.

Of course, his mom didn't like Alice, complained she was a schemer who took up too much of his time, but Mike neither confirmed nor denied it. Instead, he led her to the living room where he'd set his open textbook, with the pretense of studying, on the coffee table. He turned on a lamp to dispel the growing rainy-day shadows. Behind him, Alice drew in a tiny yet noisy breath and walked to the shelves housing the dolls. He watched Alice take in the collection, saw her rub her arms as if to force the goosebumps back under her skin.

"They're watching me," she said. "It's creepy."

Since the dolls had always been there, Mike never noticed if they were creepy or not. They were just a part of the room. Now, he studied them, trying to see them through Alice's eyes. Within the menagerie of glass eyes, he saw his shadowy reflection, ghost-like, looking back at him. It made him feel hollow and insubstantial and he shivered under their reflective gaze.

"They're not that bad," he said hiding his discomfort. "And this is only part of the collection. She has a whole room downstairs where she keeps the special ones."

"What sort of special ones?"

"Dunno. Never been in the room, she'd kill me if I had."

A little smile flickered across Alice's lips and danced in her eyes.

"Will you show me?" Alice asked. "Might be kinda fun in a scary movie way."

Years of being told the room was off-limits gave him a moment's hesitation, but Alice wanted to see it. Besides, his mom wouldn't be home for hours and, another bonus, he might get the opportunity to cop a feel.

"Sure," he said and put his arm around her. "If you get scared, I'll keep you safe."

"Will you now?"

"What? Don't you think I can protect you?"

Alice squeezed his butt and said, "Maybe you'll be the one needing protection." Then she pulled back and slid her hand into his as he struggled to keep his growing erection from becoming noticeable. "Lead on."

Mike guided Alice down to the basement and room with the green door. The brass knob was cool under his hand as he turned it, then stopped short of completely unlatching the door. If his mom were to come home now, he'd be in deep shit. He started to change his mind about the whole idea, maybe take Alice to his room instead, but the heat radiating from her made his mind up for him. Also, her unspoken intention lent a layer of thrilling danger that caused the front of his jeans to tighten again. In his sudden haste, the door banged against the inside wall and bounced back. He caught it before it shut and pushed it open. Slow this time.

Not stopping to give the dolls a cursory glance, Alice stepped up the slight rise and into the room. She turned to him and stripped off her shirt, her nipples hard against the filmy material of her bra. He felt the pressure build in his throat and assumed he moaned when she undid the buttons on her jeans. His feet carried him into the room, his hand reached around to caress her lower back then drew her into him. Lips met, tongues slid against each other, and hands fumbled to undo clothing and simultaneously stroke skin. They lowered onto the carpeted floor and continued their exploration of the other's body, hers wet and soft, his hard and slick. The weight of the dolls' stares went ignored.

Mike rolled Alice onto her back and the wheeled leg of one of the bassinets standing in the middle of the room got in the way.

"Sorry," he mumbled into her neck as he pushed the bassinet aside.

She responded with a low giggle and ran a hand along his ribs, raising the flesh in a rolling wave of goose pimples. So lost in Alice, the sound of crunching dirt outside the room didn't register with him, but the screechy voice did.

"Michael Waylon Connors!" his mom said with enough force in her words to cause his muscles to lock up.

The initial paralysis broke. He frantically grabbed his shirt and covered himself as, languid, Alice pulled on her top, a smirk on her face.

"Hello, Mrs. Connors," Alice said, struggling with her jeans.

"Don't 'hello' me, missy." His mom walked into the room and looked back and forth between them, glaring at Alice each time. "And just what was going on here?"

Mike stared dumbfounded as he watched Alice flip her hair out of her eyes like they had been caught doing nothing more than holding hands.

"You know," Alice said. "You just want to make us say it so you can shame us."

"Don't propose to know my mind, little girl." She turned to Mike, who felt trapped between two opposing forces. "Michael, you and your little whore get your asses out of this room."

That word, whore, pissed Mike off and, despite feeling vulnerable in his nakedness, he turned on his mom.

"You won't talk about Alice that way. I love her," he said. Although it wasn't what he expected to say but since it was the truth, he went with it.

He chanced a peek at Alice who looked back at him with her head tilted to one side and a thoughtful smile on her face. Alice, button fly still undone and shirt inside out, stole out of the room. After picking up the rest of his clothes, he strode out after her but a firm grasp on his arm stopped him.

"I'm not done with you. Wait for me in the kitchen," his mom said.

Giddy from the confrontation and admission of love, Mike pulled out of her grip and went to Alice. Together they started for the stairs, together they heard Mike's mom crooning to the dolls that it was going to be okay, the naughty teenagers were gone.

ಬೊಂಜ

A week later, Mike lay on his back in bed wishing he could go see Alice, but his mom had forbid them from getting together and had gone so far as to talk with Mike's boss, Mr.

Hamilton, to make doubly sure they stayed apart. She'd even installed a shiny new padlock on the door to the room of dolls, like he'd ever go in there again anyway. The argument that'd ensued after the incident left him feeling guilty at the pain he'd caused his mom, but, God, how he wanted Alice. Seeing her at school wasn't enough, but sneaking out wasn't an option. His mom had taken to sleeping in the living room like a guard. He felt no matter what he did, it wouldn't be the right thing and someone would get hurt. The sharp rattle of pebbles on his window shattered his miserable thoughts.

He pushed himself up onto his elbows and looked out into a night lit by the full moon. Alice stood, hair like liquid silver, with one hand on her hip and the other hanging loosely by her side. When she noticed him in the window, she motioned him to come down. There was excitement in the gesture. Slowly, he pushed the window up while hoping it wouldn't make a sound. It didn't disappoint.

"Come on down," Alice said in a stage whisper. "There's something I want to show you."

"I can't. Under house arrest," he replied in the same type of whisper.

"Sure you can. Climb out your window and onto the porch roof. It's not that far of a drop."

He'd never thought of that, and she was right, it wouldn't be a big jump to the ground. First, though, he looked back at his closed door and listened for his mom. The muted sounds from the TV were all he heard. *Good, she's downstairs.* He swung a leg over the sill and, once his foot was firmly planted on the asphalt shingles, his body followed. Cool sea air teased his skin and he thought about going back for a sweater but decided against it. Why chance being discovered?

The gritty shingles squeaked under the weight of his heels as he shuffled to the edge of the porch roof then squatted. In the silvery light, the gutter was bright white and didn't appear to be very secure but he didn't see anything else to use to swing down. He grabbed the gutter's lip then pushed off. For a moment he hung, shoulders screaming at the awkward angle, before he let go. His feet hit the ground with enough drive to send shock waves through his knees and knock him on his ass. Alice laughed. Mike froze.

"Shhhh," he said as the wet grass soaked through his jeans. "She'll hear you."

When she'd contained the giggles, she replied, "Doubt it. She's watching TV, I checked. Besides, she doesn't scare me." Alice held out a hand to help him up. "Come on."

They ran down the street. The crash of waves thundered in time to their footsteps. They slowed when they came to the main road. Alice crossed, then disappeared into the brush.

"Wait," he said. "Where are we going?"

"You'll see," she said as she pulled a flashlight out of her hoodie pocket and turned it on. "It's not far."

Mike followed. Twigs snapped underfoot and the thin branches of saplings slapped Mike in the chest but he soon caught up to Alice, who stood on one of the hiking trails that traversed the forest and began somewhere near the bridge. She bounced from foot to foot while waiting but took off again when she saw him. The moonlight filtered through the overhead branches and cast alternating pools of silver and pockets of shadow as they walked in silence. Their feet crunched on last autumn's fallen leaves as insects hummed and, in the distance, an owl hooted. Mike wondered where she was taking him then Alice veered off the path.

She led him through the ferns and bramble into a clearing where a blanket lay under a magnolia tree surrounded by soft moss. A picnic basket sat on the blanket. The river flowed steadily past, its water burbling against exposed stones that stretched from bank to bank like turtle's backs. Alice sat on the blanket and rested against the tree trunk.

"Isn't it wonderful? A magnolia tree growing where it normally wouldn't," she said.

He didn't know what to say, all the excitement and sneaking out for a stupid tree left him disappointed. The wonder on her face, however, made him smile and he felt her awe made it worthwhile. But, then again, she'd packed a picnic so it wasn't only about the tree.

"Come on, silly, sit with me," she said, patting the space beside her.

Together they unpacked the basket while she admitted the midnight feast was one of the sample picnic baskets her dad had prepared for *The Crystal Palace*. She didn't think he'd miss it. While they ate, they talked about school and friends, touched and kissed, and railed against how unfair Mike's mom was being. At least she hadn't called Alice's parents and told them. When they were finished, they lay on the blanket, Alice nestled in the crook of his arm, and they watched the stars twinkle amidst the leafy branches. A quiet peace settled over Mike, usually not one for romance, and he didn't want the night to end.

"I could lay like this forever," she said making him think she'd read his mind.

"I know what you mean," he said.

"Here's a random thought, why don't we?"

He kissed the top of her head, "Because we can't."

"I didn't mean literally but why can't we?" She rolled onto her side and placed a hand on his chest. "We'll both be eighteen soon and ready to start our own lives. Because you're the one with the Harvard Law scholarship, I'd follow you. I can work while you go to school."

He turned the idea over in his mind. He'd been too wrapped up in enjoying his popularity, and the unfettered relationships attached to it, while balancing the work necessary to get into a good school to factor a girlfriend into the mix. But he hadn't met Alice yet, hadn't discovered love. No matter which way he spun it he discovered that he no longer envisioned himself alone. Alice fit into the scenario like it'd been predestined. Wait. Where'd that thought come from? What had happened to him? Alice happened was what.

⁖⃓

Mike, Early Spring, Present

After tucking the key back under the welcome mat, Mike decided to skip checking out work prospects at the dock and went back to Tanya's. When he walked in the door, Tanya threw herself at him and buried her head in his chest. The sugary scent of her martini rolled off her as she trembled. Mike gently held her shoulders and pushed back until he was able to see her pale face.

"What's wrong?" he asked.

"There's something fucking weird going on," she said. "I'm scared shitless, Mike, and that pisses me off. I'm not some girly-girl who frightens easy."

"Let me grab a drink then we'll sit and you can tell me what's going on," he said.

Mike moved past her to the counter. The fear in her eyes disturbed him and he needed fortification before hearing the story. He poured a couple of inches of Jack into last night's empty glass, *screw it*, he filled it to the top. Then he brought it to the table, sat, and took a healthy swallow.

"Okay, lay it on me," he said.

She twirled her martini glass as she stared into its depths like a psychic gazing into a crystal ball. Mike didn't know what she'd see there but he noticed she'd skipped the mix and drank straight vodka.

"There's strange shit going on," she said. She peeked at him from under her eyelashes, and took a deep breath when he didn't react. "My trailer's never had problems with drafts but now there's odd cold spots." She gulped back the rest of the vodka.

While she was occupied with pouring more, he said, "Could be it's just getting old."

"Maybe," she said but her voice carried a hint of doubt. "There's more. I keep thinking I see someone with blonde hair standing in the hallway." He started to say it was probably just her reflection but she cut him off. "And it's not my reflection. I don't have a mirror in the hallway. And sometimes I smell vanilla and musk and green apples. I don't even have musk."

Suddenly, Mike drained his glass, the Jack burning in his throat and the familiar buzz alighting in his brain. He got up to pour another while his mind refused to believe what Tanya was saying. Alice never bothered his other girlfriends—might as well call it what it was—why would she start now? He brought the bottle back to the table with him.

"It's probably nothing, Tanya," he said. "Except for an overactive imagination, maybe."

A nerve in her jaw twitched and she said, "Don't tell me I'm crazy. I'm not. I know what I saw and smelled."

"I didn't call you crazy. I meant there has to be some logical explanation. That's all."

"Alright then, Mr. Smartypants, explain away the voice that told me 'He's mine'."

Mike couldn't, so he said nothing.

"Did you ever find Alice?" she said.

Jack sloshed onto the table as Mike's hand started to shake and his stomach plummeted at the unexpected change of direction.

"What does she have to do with anything?" he said. The tone of his words came out sounding angrier than he meant them to.

"Nothing. Everything. I don't know," she said. "For some reason that bitch popped into my head."

He slammed his glass on the table and said, "Don't you call Alice a bitch. Just because you never liked her doesn't mean she was."

A mean expression crawled across Tanya's face, it tugged her lips into a snarl and narrowed her eyes until they looked more cunning than sexy. She took a slow sip of her vodka then swirled the remainder around the glass.

"She was a whore. It's better that you didn't find her," she said, then almost as an afterthought added, "bet you didn't know she was humping Jay."

Her words crushed his heart and booze-fueled rage oozed out.

"Don't you say that. Jay tried to force himself on her. I caught him at the bonfire," he said. "Remember that night? I rescued her."

Tanya laughed, a callous sound like crows on a wire, then said, "Really, Mike? Don't tell me after all this time you still believe she was the victim?"

That's not how it went, it couldn't be. Tanya lied. Alice would never have faked something as horrible as rape.

"You're wrong about Alice." He pounded the table with his fist. "Why couldn't you all see who she really was?"

Mike shot out of the chair, it bounced against the floor before clattering to a stop, and strode to the door. She didn't try to stop him.

"Maybe it was you who couldn't," she said to his back.

"You're full of shit," he said and went out the door.

Her glass smashed against the door as he slammed it shut and jogged down the drive to his car. He glanced over his shoulder and saw Tanya standing in the doorway. She leaned against the jamb, the scared look back on her face, then noticed him watching.

"Asshole!" she yelled, then went inside.

For a moment Mike felt bad for her but it passed and he got in the car.

ଛୀଓଷ

Sue, Early Spring, Present

Sue placed her keys in the bowl, and a sense of disturbance settled over her. *Someone's been here.* Not bothering to remove her shoes and coat, she headed for her children, her babies. She wanted to make sure they were okay before going through every room to see if anything had been stolen. In a way, she felt like the three bears must have upon coming home and discovering someone had been there.

At the bottom of the stairs, she noted the duvet was gone and footprints led to the laundry room and back. She crept into the room and saw the duvet on top of the washing machine. *Now who'd do something like that?* Like they caught her thoughts, her children whispered, *the big boy was here.* For a second, she had no idea who they were talking about then it came to her. *Michael.* So, he'd stopped to pay her a visit. She hadn't been home, but maybe he'd return. Her heart warmed at the prospect. The padlock rattled.

Sue jumped. She watched as the lock bounced up and down like someone tested its strength. Then it stopped. She frowned and wondered if she'd really seen the lock move. Her children started to whimper and it didn't matter if the lock had moved or not. She went to the door, unlocked it, and marched inside. It clicked shut behind her.

ॐ

Mike, Early Spring, Present

Blood roiling, Mike sped down the road. He knew he shouldn't be driving but *The Dirty Birdie* was only a block from Tanya's. As he pulled in, he questioned whether he should go back. Tanya had honestly been terrified and probably hadn't meant what she'd said. But then again he believed *a drunk man says what a sober man thinks*, and who better to identify with it than him.

When Mike stepped into the pub alone, John raised an eyebrow at him while he mixed drinks for the early dinner crowd. A slim, dark-haired server flitted from table to table chatting and smiling as she collected plates and glasses. Conversation all but drowned out the music. Mike scanned the room and took the empty stool at the far end of the bar, away from everyone else. John called out that he'd be right there as Mike settled into the stool. He swiveled the seat so the wall was at his back and waited.

"Whiskey and draught?" John asked while he wiped the bar with a cloth then set down a coaster.

"Jack, double, straight up," Mike said.

"Rough night?" John said.

"You could say that."

John looked at him as if debating whether to say something else or not then the chatter of the bar printer took him away.

When he came back, he placed Mike's drink on the coaster and said, "First one's on the house." Then went to read the printer chit before Mike could say thanks.

Damn Tanya and her lies. Adrienne's voice, soft with the cadence of youth, floated from the recesses of his mind. Hadn't she told him the same things? Had they all known something about Alice he didn't? Not possible, they had to be wrong. Hadn't they? Of course they were, he was the only one who really knew Alice.

Alice sat on the stool beside his.

"Tanya has been spreading lies about you," he said. "She's saying you hooked up with Jay. That he wasn't trying to force himself on you."

"You know the truth, so what does it matter what Tanya says?" Alice asked.

ಬಂ ಅ

Mike, Mid Spring, Senior Year, 1992

Head down, Mike paced under the magnolia tree. Every time the breeze blew through, it stirred the leaves and the rain collected on them sprinkled down. As a fresh shower of water dripped down the back of his neck, Mike flexed his hands. Branches cracked somewhere nearby and he snapped his head up to scan the forest. *Where was she?* A squirrel broke cover, raced along the edge of the clearing, then launched itself onto a nearby tree. Mike resumed his pacing.

Soon a little ditch in the moss stretched from one side of the clearing to the other and still no Alice. Mike did an about face and almost knocked her over. She jumped out of the way, her laughter startling the squirrel into scolding her.

"I'm so sorry," she said when she controlled her amusement. "But you should have seen the look on your face." Her words sent her into another round of giggling.

He felt his face flush and he snapped at her, "What's with this bullshit rumor? You sleeping with Jay?"

The mirth strangled in her throat and she froze. Angry blood thrummed through his veins as his muscles tensed, he stood his ground. Her eyes ticked back and forth across his face like she was reading him. He frowned at her.

"Well, I'm waiting," he said. *Please say it's not true.*

"Who told you that?" she asked and took a step back while crossing her arms across her chest.

"Does it matter?" *Please say it's not true. Please.*

"It does to me. I want to know."

"Adrienne might have. And Jay." He held his breath.

Alice cocked a hip to the right, "Look at the sources. Tanya's best friend, who hates me because Tanya does, and the guy who tried to rape me. Don't tell me you actually believed them?"

The tension drained and Mike relaxed. When she put it that way, yeah, it sounded kinda lame.

"After what happened, I don't know why you still hang with them anyway," she said.

"Jay said it was all a misunderstanding and he was sorry," Mike replied.

"Yeah, he would. Asshole."

"Besides, we've all know each other since we were little." Mike pushed the latest attack of water droplets from his hair. "They're my friends."

"But do you believe them? Do you believe that I could honestly sleep with Jay?"

It was Mike's turn to scan her face in an attempt to see whether she told the truth or not.

"Oh come on! I would never fuck around on you, especially not with Jay." She came over, wrapped her arms around him, and leaned her forehead on his chest. "I love you, and only you. What about our plans?"

She made sense, why would she throw what they had away? He hugged her in return.

"I'm sorry. I didn't believe them, but I had to ask," he said.

"Don't you trust me?" Her voice sounded like she might cry anytime.

"Of course, I trust you."

"More than your friends?"

"More than them."

She turned her head so she looked up at him, "Would you stop hanging out with them? For me?"

Mike hesitated then said, "How about I stop hanging out with them as often?"

"I can deal with that." She snuggled back into his chest. "Just promise me that if they say anything else, you trust me. They don't know me like you do."

"I promise."

૭൯ർ

Mike, Early Spring, Present

"Mike Connors!" a booming voice cut through the noise.

Mike turned and saw a balding Andrew with a mousy woman in tow striding his way. *Great, someone else to ask about Alice.*

"Andrew, good to see you," Mike lied as they shook hands.

"You, too. When did you get back?" Andrew said.

"Little over a week ago. How's things?"

From there the rest of the evening passed in an alcohol hazed reminiscence while the mousy woman, Andrew's wife Helen as it turned out, kept nudging Andrew and telling him it was time to go. He laughed her off and told her he hadn't seen Mike in almost twenty years then ordered another Jack for Mike and virgin Caesar for himself. By the time John yelled out last call, Mike was feeling pretty good especially since Andrew hadn't once asked about Alice.

He called John over to see how much he owed.

"Andrew took care of it," John said as Mike slipped his keys out of his pocket. John leaned his palms against the bar. "You're not thinking of driving are you?"

"I'll be fine. I'm not going far," he replied.

"Sorry, can't let you do that. Hand over your keys. You'll thank me in the morning." John, all business now, held out his hand for the keys.

"Really, I'm okay."

The smack of John's palm hitting the bar silenced the room. Mike felt all eyes turn toward him, bore into him, and his face flushed.

"Keys. Now," John said. Mike stalled, more from being startled than from not wanting to relinquish them. "Don't make me call the cops."

Having John call the cops was the last thing Mike wanted.

He tossed them over. John plucked the keys out of the air and smiled.

"That's better," he said. "Want me to call the cab?"

Wanting to get out of there, out from under the stares, Mike said, "No, thanks. I can walk." Then wound his way out of the pub and into the night.

At some point the wind had picked up, it ruffled his hair and slithered its way through his shirt. He shivered and cursed the lack of foresight to grab a jacket, but he'd left in a rush. Thankfully, it wasn't raining. A car passed him. The exhaust fumes trailing in its wake covered the hint of salt that hung in the air. With nowhere else to go, and he refused to call his mom to come get him while he was in this condition, he trudged in the direction of Tanya's. He hoped she wouldn't still be angry or wanting to talk about Alice.

Mike came here to put the past to rest, put Alice to rest, sober up, and figure out how to fix the mess he'd made of his life. Damn Tanya, and her seductive offer. If he'd found somewhere else to stay, he might have things almost sorted out by now. But, no, he had to go and move in with her and shoot his resolve to sober up to shit.

Pebbles scrunched under foot as he stumbled up the drive. A light burned in the living room, its glow throwing an amber square onto the weedy lawn. Praying she hadn't locked him out, he turned the knob. He said a silent thanks as it opened with ease and he stepped inside to silence. It draped over him, made him uneasy. He expected Tanya to be waiting, and, depending on her mood, ready to make up, or start another fight. Maybe she'd passed out already, a likely plausibility.

He tiptoed down the hallway, Haywire mewed at the closed bathroom door, and into the bedroom. In the semi-dark room, he made out a shape on the bed and assumed it was Tanya. He relaxed. There'd be no more fighting today, and, when he thought about it, no making up either. Weary, he undressed then padded to the bathroom for one last piss before bed. He pushed the cat with his foot, and opened the door.

Steam floated out carrying the aromas of vanilla and musk and green apple with it. Tanya must have had a shower before bed and forgot to turn the fan on, so when he walked inside he flicked it on. The whirr and sporadic ting of a bent blade filled the room. He lifted the lid of the toilet then the splatter of liquid hitting liquid competed with the fan. As he scratched his ass, he glanced at the mirror above the sink. Urine spurted out of him once, twice, then dried up at the words written on the steam-misted mirror: *He's mine.*

His legs tottered and he blindly reached out to grasp the shower curtain in an attempt to stay standing. The rings clattered against the bar and a foot, toenails painted cherry red, emerged. A relieved laugh rose from his belly.

"Ha, ha, Tanya," he said. "Nice touch with the mirror." Then he pulled the shower curtain all the way back.

Tanya's head rested against the wall, her arms floated in the crimson water, a razor sat on the edge in a pool of pink water. His heart stopped. Bone numbing cold swaddled him in its embrace as he dropped to his knees. Acting on instinct, he put a finger on her neck to check for a pulse. Under her tepid skin, he felt a weak flutter growing weaker with every throb. He shot to his feet and raced out of the room in search of the phone.

Shortly after placing the *911* call the trailer became the center of hurried activity. Paramedics quickly assessed the situation and worked to stabilize Tanya while Mike paced the hall. They told him she'd slashed across her wrists instead of wrists to elbow and it was probably what kept her alive for so long. But she was lucky he'd come home when he did, any later and she'd have died. Then they whisked her away and Mike slouched into the living room.

An officer came into the room as Mike sat. He thought he recognized the young man lurking in the older man's face.

"Jay?" Mike said. He was the last person Mike expected to see in a uniform.

"Sherriff McVey now but Jay's good enough for old buddies," Jay said. Then his face took on a solemn cast. "I'm sorry, but I have to ask you a few questions."

Mike answered as best as he could given his dazed state while Jay took notes. No, he didn't know why Tanya wanted to kill herself. Yes, they'd been living together. No, he'd spent the evening sitting in *The Heron's Roost* because they'd had a fight. No, it hadn't gotten violent. Yes, he remembered what it was about, the fight was about Alice.

Jay paused at that then snapped his notebook shut and said, "That's all I need for now. I'll be in touch to let you know how Tanya is and if I have anymore questions." He leaned against the doorjamb, all friendly now. "I wouldn't recommend staying here tonight. Is there anywhere else you can stay?"

Alice sat down beside him and said, "Go home."

"Yeah, my mom's," Mike said. "But my car's at the pub." If his emotions weren't so deadened, he'd be embarrassed.

"Come on," Jay said. "I'll give you a ride out to her place."

ﾂﾂﾂﾂ

Mike watched the rain flash like liquid diamonds in the cruiser's headlights as they receded. Then turned and knocked on the door. He didn't have to knock again. The door opened and his mom, wearing a purple housecoat, stood there backlit by the foyer light. Other than a few more wrinkles around her green eyes and a touch more grey in her hair, she'd remained remarkably the same.

"I heard," she said and opened her arms. He stepped into them. "I'm so sorry, Michael." Then she pushed him away. "This all could have been avoided if you'd come straight home in the first place."

"Not now, Mom," he said and brought his bag inside. "Please, not now. I just want to sleep."

"Don't let me stop you," she said. "I've been waiting for you for twenty years, what's one more night?" The force of her sarcasm had no effect on him.

He went around her and his mom huffed then shuffled to the kitchen. He climbed the stairs with one hand gripping the banister as if to pull himself up the steps. They groaned in the same places he remembered from childhood, the places he avoided when he snuck out as a teenager. At the top, a night-light cast the hallway in a mosaic of light and dark. A patina of dust coated the glass of the needlepoint pictures adorning the walls. A small table, the twin of the one in the foyer, held a vase of dried flowers. To his immediate right lay the bathroom and his mom's room. Across from the bathroom was the guestroom then his old room. All the doors were open except his.

Mike walked along the runner of blue carpet, the center of which was worn to a pale blue, and into the guest room. He flicked the switch to turn the overhead light on. A bed, dresser, and nightstand with a lamp on it gave the room a monastic look, like his mom didn't want her guests to become too comfortable. The browns and beiges added to the impression. *Welcome home.*

Dropping his bag to the floor, he turned the light back out, and flopped onto the bed. For a moment the room spun, he put a foot on the floor to steady it. In the darkness, he avoided thinking of Tanya, instead the blonde of Alice's hair shone in his mind's eye and she whispered for him to meet her at the magnolia tree. The wind howled alongside the house, whistled past the window. Its mournful song sounded like a crying baby. Goosebumps marched down his spine and he dropped off into sleep to dream of razors and dolls and Alice. The soundtrack of wailing infants played in the background.

ଔଔ

Sue, Early Spring, Present

Sue leaned against the counter. Aromatic steam rose from the coffee mug in her hand and filled the kitchen with its comforting odor. Last night's storm had blown away and left behind the kind of grey day to make everything appear swaddled in wet cotton. She blew on her coffee making little ripples on the surface, took a sip, then set the mug down to lift the flying pan out of the cupboard. As she set it on the burner, motion outside drew her attention. A rust-bitten blue vehicle—she wasn't familiar with the different makes and models—pulled into the drive followed by the Sherriff's. Sue watched Deputy Truss get out of the blue one and into the cruiser then they drove away. She figured they must have been dropping off Michael's car.

What was she going to do with him? Her emotions traded places as quickly as patchy clouds crossed the sun on a windy day. She fluctuated between wanting to hate him for leaving her as his father had, smothering him with love, and screaming at him for taking so long to come home. Might as well add cry for him while she was at it. By the state he'd showed up in last night, the rumors of there being a new drunk in town were true. Michael's father had been an alcoholic, and so had his dad before him, so it wasn't a surprise.

Sue had no idea where Denis, Michael's father, was and stopped caring a long time ago. Now he was a distant figure who had drank and railed against her whenever she left to deliver a baby. He never did approve of her as a midwife, thought it on par with witchcraft, and even went as far as to accuse her of purposely miscarrying their first two pregnancies. They'd occurred during her last trimester and it was hard for him to understand why, after making it past the first six months, her body would reject them. She remembered coming home one day to a house in shambles and a drunk husband who ranted about not finding the potion she'd took to get rid of the babies. In hindsight, she should have walked out but then Michael came along and everything was good for a while. Another late miscarriage, however, started the cycle over until, finally, Denis found more fertile soil in the postmistress and ran away to the mainland with her. When Denis had left, Mike would have been two, not old enough to remember. But he was more like his father than he knew.

Sue turned on the burner, then took eggs out of the fridge. Might as well get the bacon from the freezer downstairs and make Michael a decent breakfast. Something to take the edge off of the hangover he'd have. Something to show she still loved him even if she didn't say it.

She made her way to the freezer in the laundry room. Maybe Michael would like a couple of fried tomatoes with his bacon and eggs. She thought she might have a jar of last summer's tomatoes left in the pantry, and there they sat next to a jar of pickled beets. As Sue grabbed them, the air in the pantry stirred. A cool breath feathered across the back of her neck, then pain ripped through her earlobe like someone had tugged it, hard. The whispering started.

Soft at first then gaining in force until the small space filled with the sounds of children yelling while the wail of infants threaded in and out. Her children, her babies, they needed her. Dismissing the pain in her earlobe, she abandoned the tomatoes and went to see what disturbed the children.

Their cries billowed out, cocooned her, as she stepped inside their room and turned on the light.

"It's okay," she said. "Mama's here."

ῴ–‑

Mike, Early Spring, Present
Mike was brushing his teeth to remove the fuzz coating them, and wondering if Tanya was all right, when the hot scent of scorching iron tickled his nose. *What the hell?* He dropped his toothbrush, dashed down the stairs, and into the kitchen. A frying pan sat smoking away on a burner orange with heat. *Jesus Christ.* He yanked it off the burner, the handle burning his palm, then tossed it in the sink where it sizzled when it hit the water. Mike waved his scalded palm in the air. Where was his mom? Leaving things unattended on the stove wasn't like her. The door to the basement opened and she emerged, her face flushed.

"You okay?" he said.

She set down a packet of bacon and said, "Fine. Just dropped a jar of tomatoes. Last one, too. Why?"

"Uh, because you left a frying pan on the burner and your face is all red."

"Took a tad longer to clean up than I thought." She poured him a coffee and handed over the mug. "And climbing up and down stairs tires me sometimes. I'm not young anymore."

Satisfied with her answer, he took his coffee to the table and watched her start breakfast. Soon the silence spun into the pop and crackle of frying bacon, the air growing greasy and fragrant.

"Anyone call to say how Tanya's doing?" he said, an unlikely prospect, but he need to ask.

She broke eggs into another pan and said, "No, but the sheriff did bring your car home. I'm assuming that's yours?"

"Blue Toyota Camry?"

"It's blue, that's all I can tell you."

"Yup, it's mine."

She pursed her lips and flipped the eggs onto a plate, then said, "I have one rule if you're going to stay here." In a rush of clarity, Mike knew what she was going to say before she did. "No drinking, Michael. I can tolerate a lot but not having an alcoholic under my roof."

Distress made his throat close, the hot coffee he'd just taken a drink of sprayed out as he coughed and sputtered.

"Sorry," he said, banging his chest with one hand and mopping up the coffee with his napkin. "Wrong pipe."

She harrumphed as she brought the breakfast to the table.

"As long as we're clear on the no booze in my house," she said.

"Yeah, I'm good with it. I was planning on quitting anyway," he said. He felt the first pangs of yearning needle at his nerves with its sharp teeth.

❧❧

Mike sat on the porch swing, resting a mug of coffee on his thigh, enjoying the combination of cool sea air and the warmth from his mug. The low cloud cover muted the gentle susurrus of waves at low tide, no gull screeched. He felt as if he sat in a world with the sound turned down low and one whose colors had been mixed with a heavy dose of grey. Off in the distance, the ferry chugged along. Salt tainted the wind and the organic scent of rotting seaweed wafted up from the beach. It was almost overpowering but, for the first time in five days, odors weren't making his stomach riot. His headache was gone, too. Though his hands did tremble slightly every now and again and when he least expected it, he broke out in sweat. He wondered how Tanya was fairing with her attempt at sobriety.

Tanya didn't have a choice, though. Once her parents had been notified, they'd made the trek up from Oregon, and hauled her back with them after the hospital deemed her fit for release. When they arrived back there, they promptly committed her in a rehab center. Last time Mike had heard from her was right before she was admitted. She told him she was never coming back to Fallen's Island and she never wanted to hear from him, her suicide attempt was his fault.

Mike took a gulp of coffee and felt the hot liquid slide down to his belly and radiate out. Now Jack, that heated him up. On the heels of the thought rode a flash of shame. He'd admit it hadn't been easy to jump on the wagon cold turkey. There'd been days, when the DT nightmares and wracking spasms left him hollow, where he'd almost caved and drove into town in search of relief. On those days, he'd find something to repair; a leaky faucet, a crack in the wall, a loose board on the porch, using the tools from the toolchest he'd discovered in the shed. He managed to make it through. However, he missed Alice, missed her presence, her comforting chatter. But this letting go was all part of her plan. Wasn't it? Part of the reason she told him to return.

An engine revving then slowing caught his attention and he saw the Sheriff's cruiser pull into the drive. His heart bumped out a hard double wham. *What the hell?* And Tanya came to mind. He stood. Images of Tanya deciding to report her suicide attempt hadn't been alcohol driven, Mike made her do it, galloped through his head. The cruiser stopped and Jay got out.

"Grey day, isn't it?" Jay said. He leaned against the bumper and crossed his arms.

Wary, Mike walked down the steps. They creaked underfoot.

"Tell me about it," he said. "What's up?"

"Not much. I was in the neighborhood and thought I'd check in on you. How's things, anyway?"

"They're good, really good despite the circumstances."

"Glad to hear." Jay uncrossed his arms and pushed off the bumper. "Adrienne wanted to know if you'd like to join us for dinner tonight? You know I married her, right?"

"Yeah, Tanya told me."

At the mention of her name, Jay looked off into the trees, and said, "I'd like to say what she did was a tragedy but something good is coming from it." Jay looked back at Mike. "At least she's getting help."

Mike didn't know if the comment was pointed or not, so he said nothing.

"Anyway, dinner's at six if you're up for it," Jay said.

Mike mulled it over, then said, "Works for me. See you then."

He watched Jay leave and wondered what he'd gotten himself into. Ever since the night on the beach, his and Jay's friendship had been shaky on a good day. But when he thought about it, dinner was probably Adrienne's idea. Jay had alluded to it.

⁎⁎⁎

"That was delicious, Adrienne. Thanks," Mike said as he carried his empty plate into the kitchen smelling of roast chicken. Pots and pans littered the countertop.

He dodged a row of dinky cars parked on the floor and stepped over a baby doll lying face down where two-year-old Alex and four-year-old Jade had left them. *Cute kids, but a handful.* Adrienne flicked on a light to disperse the deepening shadows.

"You're welcome," she said. "Here, let me take that. You go and sit down."

She took the plate with one hand and used the other to turn him around and push him in the direction of the living room. Alex roared into the kitchen, a laughing Jade close behind, and hid behind Adrienne's legs. Adrienne gave Mike a tired smile as Alex started screeching at his sister to go leave him alone. Mike walked away, he heard her referee whatever the kids were fighting about.

Mike found Jay standing at a little wet bar in the living room. The room a weird grouping of well-used furniture, state of the art TV and sound system, and prints by Monet and Munch hanging on the wall. It struck Mike as odd there'd be a bar in the living room but didn't judge.

"Brandy for dessert?" Jay asked. "Or would you rather have coffee?"

The glint in Jay's eye didn't go unnoticed and appeared, to Mike, to be a challenge.

"A brandy is fine," Mike said.

Jay smirked and poured a healthy dollop into his own glass and an inch into Mike's then handed it to him.

"To the class of '92," Jay said.

Mike recalled another such toast as they lifted their glasses and drank. The smooth brandy felt like fire and velvet going down his throat. He fought the desire to drain his glass and ask for more. Adrienne popped her head in and said she was going to bathe the kids and put them to bed. She hoped the two of them had a good chat. And, for awhile, they did. They exchanged what they'd done with the last twenty years, again Mike edited his version, as he nursed the brandy. Then Jay brought up the past, and Alice.

"What I had a hard time believing is why you'd go chasing that messed up chick after she ran away," Jay said after his fourth brandy. "I mean, she was a bitch. Accusing me of trying to rape her then screwing me behind your back."

Mike's hand spasmed. The tumbler he held fell end over end splashing brandy into the air. It landed on the carpet. Constricting bands hugged his ribs and squeezed the air from his lungs in a strangled half groan, half cough. Not trusting himself to speak, he picked up the tumbler and slammed it onto the bar. The expression on Jay's face told Mike all he needed to know, things would never be the same between them.

"Goodnight, Jay," Mike said. The words forced from between clenched teeth because attacking Jay wouldn't be a good idea. Wailing on someone in their own home would be tacky, not to mention stupid especially since that someone was the Sheriff.

"Oh, come on, Mike, don't tell me that you still believe Alice was so sweet and innocent?" Jay said.

"Give Adrienne my thanks," Mike stormed away.

The windows flanking the door rattled as Mike slammed it.

ಐಐ

Sue, Early Spring, Present

Sue sat at the kitchen table working on a crossword, a cup of tea cooling by one elbow. By the note he'd left, she knew he'd gone to Jay and Adrienne's for dinner but thought he'd be home sooner. *Must be having a good time.* She hoped he wasn't drinking with Jay, he'd done so well, but having lived with Denis made her skeptical.

The wind howled across the front of the house, it screamed past the window, and caused the rose bushes to scrape the glass. With each scritch-scratch of the branches, the temperature in the kitchen dropped. Sue shivered and started to stand, intentions of putting the kettle back on foremost, but the sound of a whisper caused her to sit back down. She waited a minute. Nothing. Positive it'd been the wind and not one of her children, she carried on.

"Miss me?" a voice said. She knew the voice.

She jumped up, her leg bumped the table and tea slopped onto her crossword. Laughter floated into the room from somewhere to the right. She snapped her head in the direction. The notes tacked to the refrigerator fluttered as if trapped in an updraft, as if someone had run past. In her peripheral vision, she saw movement and turned to track it down. She swore she saw a flash of blonde hair. Only one person she knew who'd had blonde hair that shade. Alice. Sue whipped around.

The knob on the door to the basement turned this way and that and the temperature dropped farther. Sue lightly choked on the pent-up air whooshing from her lungs. Standing in front of the door, flickering in and out of focus like a jammed piece of movie film, was Alice. She smiled at Sue then blinked out. The door flung open. *Oh no she doesn't.* Sue charged to the door, and it smacked into her shoulder as an unseen force pushed it. But she stayed on her feet and pounded down the steps as the crying began.

Not the soft cries of a lonely baby or the frenzied ones of the hungry, but howls emanating panic and fear.

ಬಾಂಡ

Mike, Early Spring, Present

When Mike walked into the house, the grandfather clock bonged one. Needing to clear his head, and fighting the urge to head for *The Dirty Birdie*, Mike had driven around the streets until after the pub had closed and the craving abated. He went into the kitchen, saw the crossword on the table, and realized his mom had probably tried to stay up and wait for him. Knowing her, she wouldn't be impressed he'd come home so late. *Hold up, why should I worry about that. I'm not twelve.* The thought smacked him upside the head and he was suddenly pissed at his mom, or maybe it was anger at Jay and his allegations about Alice feeding his emotions. His shitty life had been his mom's fault, she'd pushed Alice to run away. Not him. And if he'd started drinking because of it, because it was the only way to see Alice, whose fault was it. He needed a drink but went and took a shower instead.

Mike turned off the tap when the water faded to cold. He

snaked a heat-reddened hand out to grab the towel off the hook and gave his hair an obligatory rub before wrapping the towel around his waist. He paused in the act of opening the shower curtain. The room felt different but the why eluded him. It almost seemed as if the texture of the air had become heavy. More oppressive than anything, like someone stood on the other side of the curtain and stared at it. Had to be his mom, there was no one else in the house.

"Mom," he said. "A little privacy here."

A screech, similar to nails on a chalkboard but not quite, permeated the room. The sound set his teeth on edge, which, in turn, made him angry with her. *What the hell was she doing, and, more importantly, why?*

"Do you mind?" he said, a snarky edge to his voice.

No reply. No opening then closing of the door. He absently scratched his chest while waiting for her to either answer or leave. Despite the shower heated air, the water droplets on his skin cooled. He shivered and the squeaky smudging noise started again. *What the fuck was wrong with her?* The rings of the shower curtain clack-clacked as he drew it back. His mom wasn't there. He frowned and stepped out of the tub.

Steam swirled about the room but over by the sink, above which the mirror hung, it flowed around a clear space. The space had a vaguely human form and, as he watched, filled in. First with blonde hair then a slender frame dressed in the stylish shirt he'd first seen her wearing and jeans, but not the face. It remained a featureless visage of empty flesh. He didn't need to see the face to know whom it was but the image before him exuded the malevolence he'd felt the first night at Tanya's. This may look like Alice but there was no way it was his Alice. She only looked upon him with love, not the loathing he felt rolling off this creature. Then from one heartbeat to the next, the other Alice faded away.

Mike gawked at the spot where she'd stood. Something about the mirror caught his attention. He didn't want to look, but had to. His gaze traveled to the sink and on up to the mirror. Whatever was written on it, he wasn't able to make out from where he was, so on unsteady legs he made his way over. He bypassed the space she'd occupied, and peered at the mirror. His breath stalled as he read the two words etched into the condensation: *Find me.* Before he had time to process their meaning, drawn out squeaks echoed through the room as an unseen finger traced a symbol into the film of water:

He jumped back. The towel dropped from his waist, tangled in his feet, and, while trying to right himself, his shin hit the side of the tub. He clutched the shower curtain, rings pinging and popping as they let go under the strain. Knowing he fought a losing battle, Mike gave up and tumbled into the tub. His shoulder rebounded against the tile wall. Little white dots swarmed his vision and pulsed in time with the pain. He lay, feet hanging over the rim, at the bottom with the curtain twisted around him like a shroud.

ॐ‬ଔ

Sue, Early Spring, Present
Sue fumbled in her pants pocket for the small metal padlock key. Sweat made her fingers slick and she had problems grasping it. From behind the door, the cries of her children increased.

Help us, Mama, they yelled, the high pitched keening of infants wove around the words. Catching the key between thumb and index finger, she brought it out, but it snagged on the edge of her pocket. She scrabbled to catch it, missed, and watched the key hit the dirt floor. A small cloud of dusty dirt rose as it slid into the skim of powdery soil covering the hard-pack. Frantic, she ran her hand along where it'd dropped until she touched metal. She picked it up, rammed it into the lock, and twisted. The lock fell open. The screaming and caterwauling intensified. She turned the knob. The door reached its zenith and destruction met Sue.

Dolls lay scattered around. The glassy eyes of a beheaded bride stared up at her, arms and legs tangled together in disjointed heaps, and shreds of clothing blanketed the carpet. *Your fault, Mama*, they whispered to her. She didn't see her most prized babies among the desecration. Then Alice flickered into view. She leaned over one of the bassinets, a terrified whimper coming from it. Her hair fell like a curtain to hide her face as Alice reached in.

Anger, fear, and frustration intertwined in Sue's abdomen, she yelled, "Enough! Stop right now, missy."

Alice looked up. Sue stepped back at the obscene blank face then, bolstering her courage, came forward.

"Go away and leave my babies alone," Sue said.

Alice shook her head *no*.

Sue didn't have a clue how to force Alice to leave but she stepped into the room anyway.

Something drew Alice's attention away from Sue, she cocked her head and appeared to listen to a sound Sue wasn't able to perceive. Taking advantage of the distraction, she rushed Alice but her body passed through Alice's. Sue wheeled around, and the room was empty.

With shaking hands, Sue righted the rocking chair and collapsed into it. *My poor children. What a mess that girl made. Why now?* She didn't have an answer. If Alice had been haunting the house all these years, she hadn't shown herself. Thinking across the span of the two decades, she concluded Alice hadn't been here, this was the first time. What was different? Mike. Bolting upright in the rocking chair, she realized why Alice was back. And she thought she might know how to make Alice leave again, but was she willing to let go of Mike?

ಬಂಬ

Mike, Early Spring, Present
Mind feeling like it was full of mud, Mike lurched back to the guest room and tumbled onto the bed. He used a foot to snag his duffle bag and drew it over. The ratchet of the zipper sounded loud in the silence. Ignoring his brain's need to explore the incident in the bathroom, he dug around inside the bag until he found his jogging pants and a rolled up ratty T-shirt. The normalcy the act of getting dressed offered appealed to him. Once he'd donned the joggers, he unrolled the T-shirt and the gun hidden inside fell out to land in his lap. The metal felt cold on his skin even though he wore the pants. He didn't remember packing the handgun, thought he'd left it in Connecticut.

The night in the park seemed like a lifetime ago. Had it really been only three weeks since he flirted with ending his life? He grimaced and, not wanting to revisit the scenario again, picked up the handgun then buried it at the bottom of the bag. His mom's shadow darkened the doorway.

"You're back," she said. "Nice of you to call to say you would be home so late."

"Sorry, time escaped me," he said.

"Jay and Adrienne must have been good company."

"Uhm, dinner was okay but Jay and I had a disagreement so I drove around to calm down," he said.

She lifted her chin, and said, "I see. What did you two fight about?"

Mike rubbed his aching shoulder while debating whether to tell her the truth or not. The way she scrutinized him made him want to keep his mouth shut, but he was never good at hiding things from her.

"He was telling lies about Alice," he finally said. And hated his weakness. Again, he reminded himself he was almost forty not twelve.

"She was a trollop, Michael. Jay was doing you a favor by telling you the truth."

How would she know if Alice cheated on me or not?

"What do you know." His mom flinched and he suspected she reacted to the dismissive tone of his statement.

The atmosphere took on the electric tingle of a fight in the making. He didn't want to quarrel.

"Mom's know, they always do, especially in a town the size of this one," she said. "I said good riddance to her then and still do. She would have ruined your life."

Mike stopped working the shoulder muscle and jumped up. Adrenaline dumped into his system, his hands started to vibrate, and it blotted out his desire to keep the peace as he took a step toward her.

"How do you know what kind of life we'd have had? We could have had a great life, only you never gave us a chance.

Just scared her off." Mike realized he never knew what transpired between his mom and Alice. "What did you do to her that was so horrible she felt she had no choice but to run away?"

His mom's eyes widened when he asked the question. If it was out of surprise or fright, he couldn't be sure.

"You don't remember," she said. Her gaze flitted past him and settled somewhere near his left hip. "Don't worry about it. It's nothing." Then she turned away. "Goodnight, Michael. Sleep well." She left.

Mike followed her into the hallway, "Mom."

"What?" she said, her tone exasperated.

"If you really loved me, you'd tell me about Alice."

She hesitated then sighed and said, "I knew you were sneaking out through your window to see her so I warned Alice if she didn't leave you alone I'd get a restraining order against her. Silly little drama queen had a temper tantrum and left." Her words came out in a rush.

Her explanation didn't ring true to him, sounded practiced, but he had no proof.

"Now, if you don't mind, I'm going to bed," she said. He didn't argue. "Good night, then."

Once back in the bedroom, Mike switched off the light and lay down but sleep eluded him. Too many emotions crowded each other, too many thoughts spun through his mind, and he wondered if the message written on the bathroom mirror meant to find the truth. Find the reason why Alice ran away and, in doing so, find her. Not being able to remember what sent Alice running troubled him. He remembered everything else about that spring. Why not that?

৪৩

By the time he'd rolled out of bed the following morning, his mom had already gone to work. Good, he hadn't wanted to rehash last night. She'd left a shopping list on the fridge, for him he assumed. Another bit of luck, he would have something to do instead of dwell on the events of last night. So here he was, elbows on the handle of a shopping a cart, shoulders rolled forward, navigating the busy aisles of *Eugene's Market*. He figured it had to be a payday or something.

Three ladies his mom's age, looked his way as he pushed his cart into the soup aisle. He stopped and eyeballed the varieties, looking for the mushroom soup his mom had on the list. From his periphery, he saw the ladies lean toward each other and sneak conspiratorial glances his way. Although he didn't remember their names, he vaguely recognized them. He ignored them until he heard his mom's name mentioned.

"Yes, I think that is Sue's boy," one of the women said.

Mike shifted to the right so he could see them yet appear to study the soup cans.

"Sandy from my book-club mentioned he was back and living with Tanya," the thin woman with glasses perched on her nose said.

"Not anymore. Tanya went a little cuckoo and her parents took her to live with them in Oregon. Poor thing," another woman said. By her rigid stance and authoritative tone of her voice, Mike guessed she was the ringleader.

The rotund woman in purple clucked and shifted her basket from one hip to the other then said, "Wonder what he's doing back?"

"Obviously, he didn't find that girl he'd gone running after," the ringleader said. "What was her name again? Agnus…Abigail…Oh, Alice, that's it. Her poor parents losing her like that and with the rumor she was expecting, too. They were nice folks."

What the fuck? Alice hadn't been pregnant. The colors on the labels swirled together, and his breath wheezed. No, those gossipy bitches were wrong. Alice would have told him.

"Maybe he did find her. Maybe she's up at Sue's place now with the child," glasses said.

"Couldn't be, Mable, he…" Mike didn't hear the rest of the sentence as he'd whipped his cart around and strode out of the aisle.

Mike dodged shoppers standing about as he cursed the women and their lies. There was no way she'd been pregnant. She wouldn't keep something like that from him, they'd loved each other too much for secrets. God, he needed a drink or two or three. Keeping his eyes forward and shoulders back, he hurried through the store to the liquor section. He heard his name called once, but ignored it and kept going. Halfway down the hard alcohol aisle, he snagged a bottle of Jack. Guilt reared but he stomped it down and headed to the till.

The line up at the two open tills snaked around almost to the produce section but the *Express Lane* was near empty. He abandoned the cart and joined the queue. *Hurry up, hurry* then he was paying for the Jack and nearly sprinting out the door. The Camry's tires chirruped on the wet pavement as Mike hit the gas and tore out of the parking lot. The car fishtailed and Mike adjusted the wheel, brought it back under control, then rocketed toward home.

⁖₳

Sue, Early Spring, Present

Sue sat in the rocking chair and watched over her tattered children. Last night, she'd put them back together the best she could and set them in their proper places on the shelves. Gone were the clothes, they were beyond repair. She'd have to purchase new outfits and an arm here, a leg there, and let's not forget a missing eye or two. Thank God, Alice hadn't touched the ones in the bassinets. Those three were irreplaceable.

Her jaw clenched at the thought of Alice. She wouldn't let the girl take away her most special babies. Oh my, wouldn't Alice be surprised the next time she showed herself and Sue sat waiting, watching, guarding. And this time, Sue was prepared. She clung to the revolver she'd found searching Mike's bag for booze while he slept. Her lips pulled into a smile resembling the rictus grin of a skull.

৪৩

Mike, Early Spring, Present

When Mike walked into the house, his hands had begun to shake and a headache threatened. He kicked off his shoes, and dropped his coat on the floor. A voice in his head pestered him, reminded him of his mom's rule but he was beyond caring right now. If she caught him, then he might have something to worry about. He headed upstairs to his old room. There was something alternately comforting and sneaky about hiding in his room with the Jack.

Hand on the doorknob, he paused and stared in disbelief. She'd painted it green, too. He shivered. *What was with her painting the doors to match her doll room one?* Then he opened it and stepped inside into the scent of old books, dust, and bygone adolescent sweat.

Unlike the rest of the house, she'd changed his room. He remembered clothes had lain strewn about the floor along with a couple of crusty towels. The dresser drawers were usually half-cocked open with a lone sock or boxers hanging half in and half out of the top drawer. Papers, books, and cassette tapes had covered the top of the dresser and nightstand but at some point, she'd cleaned the room. She'd made the bed, too. Oddly, she'd left the posters of the half-naked girls she'd hated. They hung, their smiles faded and corners curled with age, in their usual spots. She hadn't kept it up, though. Cobwebs joined the books on the shelf to the few academic trophies, making them look like a chain of mismatched paperdolls.

He fell onto the bed like he'd done so many times as a teen and propped a pillow on the headboard then leaned back. Off came the safety plastic, off came the cap. He downed a healthy slug then another and another until the voices of the nattering ladies quieted. His hands stopped their jittering and the headache receded. A couple of more slams knocked down the memory of the bathroom episode threatening to come forward. Soon a warm boozy haze settled into his mind. No more worries, no more thinking, just free floating on a soothing wave. He'd missed this and wasn't able to remember why he ever wanted to give it up. Alice sat on the foot of the bed.

Mike took in her appearance and was relieved to see that she was back to normal. He didn't care for the other Alice, she scared him.

"Hey, you're pretty again. What was up last night?" he said. "Never seen you like that before, but never seen you when I'm sober. I don't think I like you when I'm sober."

Alice frowned and said, "That wasn't me."

"What?"

"Wasn't me. I can only visit when you drink."

Her confused tone cut through the calming fog and raised questions he didn't want to evaluate. He tipped the bottle and let more Jack slide down his throat.

"People are lying about you again," he said and adjusted the pillow. "Why are they always saying shit about you?"

"What are they saying this time?"

"That you were pregnant. Fuckers." Mike banged his fist on the bed. "You would have told me if you were. You wouldn't hide something like that."

"Of course not, my love. But maybe there's something you don't remember."

He pointed his finger at her, "My mom said that last night, too. What is up with you people? You're all starting to piss me off. I know what happened. We fell in love, my mom hated you so much you ran away. End. Of. Story."

A pocket of cold caressed Mike. Alice's eyes widened like she saw something he didn't then she disappeared. Mike rapidly blinked as his muddled mind attempted to comprehend her departure. Suddenly the other Alice stood beside him, face a smooth blank of pink skin, and she placed her hands on either side of his head. A deep cold permeated from her touch, it felt like the inside of his skull was frosted with ice. He jerked back, his head hitting the headboard. His hands twitched. The bottle fell from his grasp and bounced off the mattress onto the floor. Amber liquid pooled on the carpet and tainted the air with its spicy aroma. His heels drummed on the bed, then he stilled as his muscles locked in paralysis.

Although her face was devoid of a mouth, he heard her say,

"You will remember."

ಐ ೞ

Mike, Late Spring, Senior Year, 1992

Alice sat on his bed, her back resting against the wall beside the window, and her legs straight out but crossed at the ankles.

"I'm pregnant," she said.

Mike stopped picking at a loose thread on his bedspread, listened to the silence of the house, and wondered if he should run away. Alice reached out and traced a pattern on his arm. He marveled at the way the sun made the little hairs shine like filaments of gold.

"Did you hear me?" she said.

"Are you sure?" he said and pulled his hand away.

"Positive. I took a test." She ran a hand through her hair and watched the strands fall. "I stole it. Didn't want to buy one and have everyone finding out."

"Is it mine?" The words tumbled out unbidden. Inside he cringed. *Stupid move, Mike.*

Alice shot him a black look and leaned over to hit him on the shoulder. He grunted under the force.

"Of course it's yours, idiot. Who else's would it be?" She trailed off as if in thought. "Don't tell me you think it's Jay's? You can't be that stupid."

He hadn't meant to insinuate he suspected it might not be his but like a dummy he couldn't drop it.

"What am I supposed to think?" he said. "Everyone, even Jay, said you two slept together. Maybe it's true. You and me used protection..."

Alice chewed on her bottom lip, appearing lost in thought,

then said, "No, I didn't sleep with Jay. But that first night with Jay on the beach, he wasn't exactly forcing himself on me. I wanted you, you weren't there, but he was. I was drunk. And when I saw you, I kinda freaked out."

A vein in his temple throbbed as he attempted to bite back the anger.

"But, I'm telling you the truth when I say I haven't slept with him," Alice said, a pleading note in her voice. "Please believe me."

Mike watched her fidget and found he did believe her. He couldn't explain it but he did. His belief, though, didn't change the fact she'd rearranged his life with two words. He saw his plans of law school slip away, saw their plans for the future crumble. This changed everything but it didn't have to.

Impulsively, Mike got up, went to his dresser, and opened the top drawer. Buried beneath his socks and underwear hid the roll of money he'd saved from his fishing job. He'd intended to use it to pay for the books his scholarship wouldn't cover. Not knowing how much Alice needed, he separated five hundred bucks from the wad and put the rest back.

"Here," he said as he held out the bills. His hand shook.

"What's that for?" she asked.

Sweat beaded under his arms and his heart raced.

"Just take it," he said. Fear and discomfort masqueraded as irritation.

"Not until you tell me why," she said in a quiet tone.

"You know why."

"No, I don't. Really. Are you saying you're breaking up with me because of what I told you?" He didn't respond. "Oh God, you are."

Tears leaked from Alice's eyes and traced black,

mascara-laden contrails down her cheeks. Mike's heart settled somewhere near his feet.

"No, no," he said. "Not that." He knew what he wanted to say but had trouble with the words. Drawing in a deep breath, he forced them out. "For, you know, taking care of it."

More tears, a slip of a sob, then she said, "I can't take care of a baby on my own. I need you."

Apparently, she hadn't heard him so he tried again, "Not for taking care of it that way. For *taking care of it*. There's got to be some place in Seattle that you can go to and they'll, you know…"

A horrified expression twisted her face into an ugly vision and the tears dried up.

"I'm not going to kill our baby," she said. "We can make this work. You'd have to attend school part-time and work part-time. Once the baby's old enough, I can find a job so you can focus on your studies. It's doable."

"Sounds like you've given this a lot of thought," he said.

"I've known longer than you."

"Can't see it working out that way. I see us trapped here on this island."

"And would there be something so wrong with that? We'd be together. What's more important, us or your proposed career?"

"You're what's important but so is being a lawyer. We don't need to have a baby right now, especially right now, we're too young. That can come later. I'm not planning on ditching you. Ever," he said.

Within the silence lying heavy in the room, a floorboard creaked out in the hallway.

"Then what are we going to do?" she said.

"Take the money, go to Seattle. It'll be better that way. You'll see," he said and waved the money at her.

She took it and said, "I'll think about it." She gazed at the bills in her hand. "Would you come with me?"

"I have to head out fishing tomorrow now that I've finished exams and I won't be back until the day before the graduation ceremony. When I get back…?"

"I don't think I could do it alone."

Mike sat beside her and pulled her into him. Her body was warm and slightly trembled and he realized she was crying again. He kissed the top of her head and murmured that everything was going to be all right while, deep inside, fear cavorted. Silently, he told himself this was the right thing to do. But, as it turned out, it wasn't.

ഇരുതു

Mike, Early Spring, Present

The other Alice released him from her freezing grip then faded away. By the tingle in his body, he knew the paralysis had broken so he rolled over to retrieve the bottle from the floor. The hairs on his arm stirred when his hand passed through the cold spot left behind by the other Alice. He grabbed the bottle by the neck and lifted it to his lips. A couple of ounces, nothing more, dribbled into his mouth. He cursed and threw the empty bottle across the room. His Alice stood in the corner.

"That other Alice lies," he said while contemplating lapping up the spilled Jack like a dog. "You weren't pregnant, were you? You'd tell me the truth."

"Maybe I'm the lie and she's the truth," Alice said. She gave him a cryptic smile before melting into the corner.

߀ড়

Mike, Late Spring, Senior Year, 1992

The fishing boat bumped against the dock and Mike jumped out to wind, then knot the rope around the metal cleat. He quickly tied rope to two more cleats, excitement over getting to see Alice quickening his hands, then he noticed Sheriff McVey stood, his arms crossed, next to the boat.

"Michael," he said. "You have a minute?"

Confused, he said, "Uh, sure. Is there something wrong?" His mom floated through his mind. "Is it Mom? Did something happen? Is she okay?"

Sheriff McVey put his hands up, palms facing Mike, and shook his head.

"Everything's good with your mom, son," he said. "I have some questions about Alice."

"Alice?" Mike said. A thousand things ran through his mind, ranging from her dad finding out about the pregnancy to her dying a slow and bloody death on a quack doctor's table. He swallowed. "Why?"

Sheriff McVey held Mike's gaze. Mike studied his friend's dad's tanned and weathered face for some clue as to what was going on. But the Sheriff gave nothing away. *Bet he'd be good at poker,* the random thought jumped into his head.

Finally, the Sheriff broke the silence and said to Mike, "I'm sorry, son, she's disappeared. Do you have any idea where she might have gone?"

Mike felt as if a tsunami had slammed into the dock. His knees wobbled and he put his hand on the creosote covered piling to stop his fall. He felt the blood drain from his face and, by the expression on Sheriff McVey's, knew he'd noticed.

"If you know where she is, Michael, don't be afraid to tell me," Sheriff McVey said. "Alice isn't in any trouble but her parents are worried."

"How long has she been missing?" Mike felt like he hovered somewhere above the scene. He heard himself ask the question but it sounded so far away.

"Four days." Anything could have happened to Alice in four long days. Black dots swarmed Mike's vision. "Are you all right?"

Sheriff McVey stepped forward and grabbed Mike's elbow. The blackness dissipated and color rushed back; the blues, greens, yellows, and browns garish in their sudden clarity. Waves shushed against the dock, ordinarily quiet and soothing, they took on the irritating quality of sandpaper on wood. A gull's screech felt like it might shatter his eardrums as the stench of diesel and seaweed made him gag. He was okay, all right.

Mike shook off Sheriff McVey's grasp then scrubbed his face with his hands feeling the prickle of a juvenile beard. His senses returned to normal, the world, however, continued to sway.

"I'm fine," Mike said, more for himself than the Sheriff.

Sheriff McVey studied Mike a beat then said, "Well then, do you know where she is?"

"Seattle, maybe? She mentioned something about going there before I left."

"Why Seattle?"

Not wanting to tell the Sheriff the truth, Mike scrambled for a satisfactory answer and settled on, "Don't know. She never said."

Another long pause, Mike tried not to squirm as he felt like an amoeba under a microscope.

"You're not hiding anything are you?" Sheriff McVey asked.

"Nope. Nothing," Mike said, avoiding the Sheriff's eyes.

"If you think of anything, Michael, any reason why she might have gone to Seattle, you be sure to let me know." Sheriff McVey took a card and pen out of his front shirt pocket, wrote on it, and handed it to Mike. "My home number is on the back."

Mike took the card. After the Sheriff extracted the promise of a call—anytime day or night—from Mike, they exchanged goodbyes and handshakes. Mike turned the card over and over as he watched Sheriff McVey walk back to shore.

₧₧

Mike, Early Spring, Present

Mike jumped up off the bed, the world teetered, and he almost lost his footing. Right before he smacked headlong into his dresser, he managed to stop his momentum and regain his balance.

"No, you're the real Alice," he said to the empty room. "You're the real Alice."

Laughter circled the room and the scent of vanilla and musk and green apples trailed behind it.

"I'll find you. I will," he said as he turned this way and that searching for Alice. "Coming back was a mistake."

₧₧

Mike, Summer, Senior Year, 1992

Graduation day came and went. Mike physically attended but his spirit drifted elsewhere and for that he was glad.

Everyone, from friends to teachers to parents, seemed to send him pitying glances, except for Alice's. Their silent accusations weighed heavy on his shoulders. He didn't even know why they bothered to attend the ceremony. Hoping she'd show up maybe? His mom sat in the front, back straight and a proud smile on her face. Alice's disappearance hadn't disturbed her in the slightest, quite the opposite. She had the gall to admit to him she was happy Alice was gone, and told him it was his chance to focus on university in the fall. They'd fought then.

July passed by on the water. Mike didn't care since the daily demands of Mr. Hamilton served to keep Mike's mind off Alice. Mr. Hamilton drove his crew hard, to the point of exhaustion most days, and Mike welcomed the nights of being so tired he fell asleep with his boots on. He wondered if they'd found Alice yet. He wondered if she'd ran away to have the baby.

By mid-August everyone concluded that Alice had run to Seattle, someone had thought they'd seen her on the ferry around the time period in question. A rumor she was pregnant started to go around and he refused to confirm it.

The end of summer loomed. Mike started his preparations for university in September and daydreamed of finding Alice. Dreamed of her showing up on the doorstep of his dormitory apologizing for the mess she'd left behind but she had to leave. He never made it to school, though. Instead, he'd tumbled down the basement steps and whammed his head with enough force to knock him unconscious for twenty-four hours. Or so he was told when he woke in the hospital with a sketchy memory and a mind full of Alice.

₧₧

"I'm leaving, Mom, I have to find Alice," Mike said.

He'd been home from the hospital less than two weeks and her image haunted him, begged him to come find her. The vision wouldn't relent, it hammered at him day and night until the only peace he received was when he was drunk. He'd slip cheap Old Man Parsons twenty bucks along with the cash needed for a bottle of the cheap stuff, a transaction making them both happy.

"You're going nowhere but university," his mom said. "She's gone. Let her go."

Mike picked up the duffle stuffed with his clothing and the money he'd made fishing. His feet thundered down the stairs, his mom's lighter patter followed as he went for the door.

"Stop this right now, Michael," she said as he reached into the bowl for the keys to his junker. "You're being foolish."

"No, I'm not." Almost to the door now.

"You haven't thought things through." She reached for his arm but he jerked out of her way.

"I have so. I can't live without Alice. I have to find her."

His mom leaned against the door to block him and said, "I know Alice is pregnant. I heard you two talking in your room that day."

Mike faltered.

"I bet the baby isn't even yours. She is a whore," his mom said.

"She's not!" he yelled, madder than he'd ever been, and slammed his fist into the wall. His knuckles felt like they were about to burst from the impact then the drywall collapsed with a crunch.

Mike pulled his hand out of the hole. It throbbed but he ignored it and, using both hands, pushed his mom out of the way. She squawked in surprise. A dull thud reached his ears. He saw her slide down the wall by the steps, tears coursing down her cheeks and dripping off her chin. They elicited no sympathy from him as he opened the door and walked out.

℠ℛ

Sue, Early Spring, Present

Crashing and banging from above invaded the quiet room. Sue looked up at the ceiling, her mouth suddenly dry, and her heart picking up the pace. She waited and listened. When the sounds didn't repeat, she got up, and went over to the bassinets. Ever so gently, she picked up the first baby, Annalise, then Isabelle, and, lastly, Elizabeth. Their desiccated bodies light in her arms as she cradled them to her chest. Even with their skin frail like ancient parchment, empty eye sockets, and lips receded into a perpetual grimace, she loved them. Loved them above all others in her collection. After all, they had once lived inside her. And she'd be damned if she let Alice take them away.

℠ℛ

Mike, Early Spring, Present

Mike stumbled out of his room, snagged his foot on the runner, and knocked over the hall table. It crashed to the floor, sending the vase tumbling through the air only to fall in an explosion of glass and dried flowers. Shards cracked underfoot as he made his way to the guestroom while mechanically whispering, *find Alice,* like a mantra. He shoveled the clothes laying about into the bag, zipped it, then slung it over his shoulder. The door banged shut. The other Alice stood there.

"I won't let you leave," she said.

She came toward him, a wintry pocket of air preceded her to envelop Mike. He shivered, remembered her frigid touch and her lies, and stepped back. Terror cleared his mind of the boozy cobwebs and, for the first time, he felt a piece of the puzzle he didn't know was missing tease the fringe of his memory. Faster than his eyes could track, she leapt forward and placed an icy hand on his cheek. And his Alice appeared.

The Alices regarded each other. The double vision made his head swim and feel as if it would split into two. Which one was the real Alice, or were they both imposters? Was his Alice still somewhere out there? While they stared each other down, he sidled in the direction of the door. Both heads swiveled his way, one blank yet impossibly full of malice, the other with love shining in her blue eyes. He stopped.

"Stay," the other Alice commanded him then turned to his Alice. "You, leave."

"As long as Mike wants me here, I'm staying," his Alice said. "He loves me."

"He doesn't love you. He loved me, you're his wishful thinking and the reason he won't remember."

Disconnected, Mike watched the exchange and, at the other Alice's assertion, saw his Alice waver out of focus. His scalp prickled. He tried to deny what he'd heard, he didn't want it to be true. It'd mean he'd spent his adult life chasing a ghost while running from…from what?

❧☙

Mike, Late Summer, Senior Year, 1992
Using the key from under the mat, Mike opened the door and went inside. An impending August storm had cut the

fishing trip short by a couple of days. He dropped his duffel full of dead fish-smelling clothes on the floor.

"Mom!" he called. "I'm back. You home?"

Only the ticking of the grandfather clock answered. *She must be at work.* He unlaced his boots, hung his raincoat, and wandered into the kitchen. The basement door hung ajar. Thinking she might be down there putting clothes in the wash or something, he went over and opened it farther.

"Mom," he called down the stairs. "Storm's on its way so I'm home early."

A plaintive shout for help drifted up the steps. *Alice.*

While he was out on the water, she'd remained silent, had stopped crying out for help or for him to come find her. Mike had begun to believe he'd finally let her go. Now she was back. The return of her disembodied voice brought with it a craving for the alcohol induced oblivion he'd grown accustomed to when she spoke. Anything to drown her out and stifle the guilt. He felt her departure was somehow his fault.

The holler came again, stronger this time, laden with fear and far too real to be his imagination. Mike bolted down the steps. His heart bang-banged with the exhilaration of finding Alice. The how and why she might be in his basement didn't cross his mind. All he cared about was wrapping her in his arms and murmuring endearments while chastising her for scaring everyone.

Dirt scrunched under his feet as he sprinted into the laundry room. The padlock on the green door to the doll room hung on the hasp by its open shackle.

"Mike," she said, her voice cracked and growing hoarse. "Help me, please."

Mike pushed the door open. *What had his mom done?* On

a little cot resting against the left wall, sat Alice wearing a billowy white nightgown he recognized as one of his mom's. Manacles encircled her wrists, stained with clotted blood in spots and weeping blood in others. Chains dangled from the cuffs and disappeared under the bed. Her hair fell in tangled knots and her pale cheeks shone with dried tears. When she saw Mike, big wrenching sobs tore from her throat. The scene short circuited his motor skills and he remained in the doorway.

When she got her crying under control, she snapped at him, "Don't just stand there. Get me outta here before she gets back."

Her tone pulled him out of the mental stall and he rushed to the cot. Alice twisted so she knelt, the nightgown stretched tight over her stomach to reveal the slight bulge of her abdomen. He marveled at the thought of life growing in her belly then she held her hands out.

"She has the key," she said and shook her hands in frustration, the chains jangling. "The last time she left me with this much extra chain, I tried pulling out the bolt under the bed but it's too tight."

"Maybe I can get it," he said as he fell to his knees and lifted the dangling sheet to peer under the bed.

The bolt sat flush with the chain links, pushing them flat on the carpet so not even a millimeter gap remained. He stretched out a hand but couldn't reach so he lay on his stomach and tried again. His fingers met the metal of the bolt. A snippet of rhyme raced into his thoughts, *righty-tighty and lefty-loosey.* He twisted hard to the left. His hand, slick with sweat, slipped and snagged on a sharp edge.

"Fucker," he said. He withdrew and stuck the offended

finger in this mouth, the salty taste of blood overran his taste buds. He removed the finger, examined the shallow cut, and deemed it not serious.

"Damn it," Alice said.

He sat up and said, "I think there's an old toolchest of my dad's around somewhere. Might have a wrench in it."

"Hurry," Alice said. "She'll be back anytime."

Mike left the room to search the basement but the toolchest proved elusive, shoulders slumped he made his way back to Alice. How was he going to free her? When he came into the room empty handed, she recoiled, and slammed her fists against her thighs.

"This is all your fault," she yelled. "You and your whack-job mom. If I'd never met you…"

Her accusation sliced him deeper than the cut on his finger.

"Calm down, Alice, I'll think of something," he said.

"You expect me to calm down? Let's trade places and see how calm you are." She started to weep silent tears. They unsettled him in a way the sobbing hadn't. "You want to know how unhinged your precious mom really is just take a look in the bassinets."

A sense of foreboding crackled in the air. Mike didn't want to go over and peek into them, didn't want to know. His feet carried him there anyway and he found himself staring at three ugly little dolls with withered arms crossed on their chests. Their skin brown like tea and peeled away in places. From their place above two small holes, empty eye sockets looked into eternity. Tiny fingernails tipped each finger and in seeing them, Mike's knees buckled slightly. *Oh my God.* And the world listed.

"Figured it out, huh," Alice said. "Yeah, she told me all about her three late miscarriages and how lucky it was for her they happened at home so she'd been able to keep them close. She said she always wanted more children."

Mike stepped back from the horrors in the bassinets. No way was his mom going to take Alice and his baby. And what about after Alice had the baby, would his mom let her go? In Mike's opinion it wasn't likely, especially if she had the capability of kidnapping Alice in the first place. He had to get Alice out of here and then find somewhere safe for them to stay. Seattle might be far enough away. *One thing at a time, first free Alice.* Sheriff McVey came to mind.

"I'm going for help," he said.

"No, don't leave me alone," she said and rose up on her knees. "Please."

"I won't be long, just going upstairs to phone Sheriff McVey. We need him."

"Hurry," she said.

Mike didn't need further encouragement, he tore out of the room, and raced up the steps two at a time. Pain rippled across the top of his foot when he misstepped and caught the underside of a stair near the top. The momentum carried him forward as his foot then his leg plunged into the dead space between the staircase and basement floor. The sudden loss of traction brought him down. He put out his hands to catch his forward descent while one leg dangled in mid-air and the other bent at an awkward angle, but completely missed the intended riser. Splinters drove into his palms as his hands skittered off the back edge of the stair. His jaw bounced against the top step with a crack sharp enough for Mike to hear with his ears and inside his head. The blackness arrived almost instantaneously to drag him into its inky depths.

‽〇℈

Mike, Early Spring, Present

His Alice stuttered, her form there one second and gone the next. Mike felt her departure in his being and knew the other Alice was right, his Alice came from him. She'd been born out of his guilt. The weight of his finally remembering, and its implications, slammed into him. *What have I done?* He already knew the answer, had at some level always known, but chose not to admit it.

All those years of searching for Alice when she'd been right here pressed down on him. All those years of smothering the guilt with his boozing, of convincing himself he needed to because it was the only way to be close to Alice forced the air from his lungs. His heart constricted. In Connecticut he'd believed he'd hit the bottom, believed he'd had nothing left, when all along he didn't have anything to begin with. Then he noticed he had the room to himself, the other Alice gone, too.

‽〇℈

Sue, Early Spring, Present

Sue sat, her little baby girls cradled in one arm. She clenched the gun with her other hand, her knuckles white from tension, and tried to look everywhere at once. Her eyes darted from the dolls on the shelves, to the door, to the corners, and briefly landed on the form on the cot. Alice wasn't going to sneak up on her watch. No, siree, she wasn't. The back of Sue's neck crawled like someone stood behind her. She whipped her head around.

Alice's empty face hovered mere inches from Sue's. She

recoiled and her bladder let go in a warm rush. Alice's chuckling, dark and full of menace, reverberated in the small room. Alice whipped around the room faster than Sue's eyes could follow and began knocking the carefully reconstructed dolls onto the floor. They thudded on the carpet. Some broke apart, arms and legs exploded from the bodies of others, and some just bounced then lay there. A glass eye rolled to a stop against the wheel of a bassinet, its dead blue iris pointed in Sue's direction.

The wetness at her crotch grew cold. Embarrassment at herself and anger at Alice brought fear and irritation to the surface.

"Tsk, tsk, you're repeating yourself, Alice," she said. "Is that all you've got?"

"No, I have you," Alice said from beside Sue. She traced the head of Elizabeth. "And your babies, you sick freak."

Sue twisted around so her shoulder blocked Alice and said, "Leave us alone."

"Like you left me alone." Alice pushed on Sue until she faced Alice again then leaned over, her nose almost touching Sue's. "Alone and scared and all because the dolls weren't enough for you, your dead babies weren't enough for you, Mike wasn't enough. Only another living, breathing baby would do."

"You were only a stupid, conniving girl who was about to ruin Mike's life. You didn't deserve a baby." Sue raised the handgun. "I did." She squeezed the trigger.

Thunder filled the room as her broken children burst into caterwauls and the babies in her arms howled. The bullet passed through Alice and thudded into the wall.

"Missed me," Alice said. "Did you miss me when I died?" She caressed baby Elizabeth's little arm. "When you came home from work and I'd gone into premature labor, how did you feel?" She wrapped her hand over the tiny skull. "Bet you didn't see that coming. Did you know it took me hours to bleed out from the hemorrhaging?" And pulled Elizabeth from Sue.

Alice dangled the withered thing, the precious baby, by its head then raised her arm as if to smash it to the floor. Sue blocked out her fear, shut down her emotions, and, with steady hands, aimed the revolver at Alice's head. If destroying the head took down zombies in the creepy TV program she'd once tried watching, it might stop Alice too. She pulled the trigger, releasing another bullet, another blast. The bullet drove into Alice's head ripping it into misty tatters that drifted above her neck stump before reforming.

"Nice try," Alice said.

Powerless to stop her, Sue watched Alice turn and slam the first baby into the wall. Sue's wail joined those of her children.

ॐ

Mike, Early Spring, Present
A boom rolled under Mike's feet and vibrated through the floor. He did a quick sideways shuffle as if the ground beneath him was too hot to stand upon. His heart missed a ka-thump. *The basement. The room.* Mike flung the door open, raced into the hallway and flew down the stairs. When he hit the foyer, the roar repeated. On this level, it sounded louder. His bruised shoulder hit the door jamb on his way into the kitchen, the force sending him reeling. Instinctively, he cupped his shoulder while darkness crept along the rim of his vision. Gritting his teeth against the sharp pangs radiating down to his fingertips, he continued through the kitchen and down the stairs.

The sense of déjà vu in reverse descended as he ran for the closed green door with its padlock hanging unlocked. He skidded to a stop. Every part of him tensed, he didn't want to go inside. Didn't want to see if the memory matched reality but, at the same time, he needed to see. From behind the door came a muffled voice. *Mom?* She was supposed to be at work. Cautious, he approached the door, turned the knob, and pushed it. He halted on the threshold. He took in the scene, his tongue drying up and sticking to the roof of his mouth.

His mom sat in a rocking chair surrounded by the wreckage of her collection. The acrid scent of gunpowder tainted the air as she cradled two desiccated dolls in one arm. *No, not dolls, her babies who'd died.* In the other hand, she held his gun and beside her stood the other Alice. The other Alice ripped the uppermost baby from his mom's clutch.

"How does it feel to have your baby stolen from you?" the other Alice said. "How about your life?"

His mom stared at him with the wide, wild eyes of the insane.

"This is all your fault," she said.

His mom placed the gun under her chin. A muffled boom resounded. Her head jerked back from the force, rocking the chair back on its runners. Rich blood, grey globules, bits of bone, and hair erupted from her split crown. They splashed the ceiling and top of the back wall in a viscous smear surrounded by fine red droplets. The gun rolled from her dead fingers. The rocking chair tipped forward, overturning Sue onto the floor where she landed in a heap.

Mike couldn't find the breath to scream, couldn't find the power to move. His mind had been wiped of thought and a part of him died. The blood and ichor started to drop from the ceiling. Runners slowly cascaded down the wall and, still, he stood immobile and empty headed.

"Mike," Alice said. "You found me."

Part of Mike woke up at her words and realized her empty face wasn't anymore. Blue eyes, a thin nose, and the pink lips he'd kissed filled the space. Though he wouldn't enter the room, his gaze flicked around, avoiding the empty husk on the floor, and settled on the cot along the left wall.

A grotesque figure lay on a white sheet gone grey with age and dust. Blonde hair capped a shriveled scalp. His eyes traced the sunken angles of her face, the lips pulled back in an eternal grin, and the empty hollows of her eye sockets. He followed the line of her neck, her ribcage, and down. Her abdomen bulged but not in the way he expected a pregnant woman's to. This wasn't the round belly of gestation but a strange figure. Finally, he found the will and stepped inside. Under Alice's gaze, he went over for a closer look and wished he hadn't.

The curled body of a wrinkled and shrunken newborn lay there with eyelids closed and concave. An umbilical cord ran from its belly, over Alice's pubis, and disappeared between her legs. The numb, distant sensation fogging his mind dissipated and returned Mike to his senses. Tears broke the image into a thousand fractured pieces.

"It was a girl," Alice said.

Images of Alice, chained and terrified, in pain with no one around to help her, played in his mind. He heard her screams, felt her fear, and smelled the copper odor of her blood. He saw Alice reach down and place the baby girl on her abdomen even as she grew weaker and weaker from the blood loss. And where had he been? Chasing a ghost across the country and committing slow suicide by bottle.

"You left me here to die," Alice said. "This is all your fault, Mike. If you hadn't left me..."

He spun around.

"It wasn't my fault, I fell and when I regained consciousness, I'd lost parts of my memory," he said. "I'm so sorry, Alice."

Alice, her body blurring, swiftly moved to his side and said, "You forgot about me."

"But I remember, now," he said. "I won't forget you again. I love you, Alice, always have. We'll stay together now, you'll see."

Mike looked at Alice, the broken babies and dolls, his mom, and his little lost one. He picked up the gun. Dust rose into the air when he laid down on the cot beside Alice, carefully moved his baby girl from Alice's abdomen and placed her on his chest.

ଓଓ

Four words, written with blood, slowly took shape on the wall:

mike & Alice forever

ABOUT THE AUTHOR

CHRIS MARRS lives on the West Coast of British Columbia. She tends bar during the day to keep her kids fed, watered, and sheltered and spends the nights writing, usually accompanied by copious amounts of coffee and sometimes a little wine. In 2012, Chris had three pieces of flash fiction published and one short story. Early 2013 saw the release of *Deep Cuts*, an anthology she edited with Angel McCoy and Eunice Magill to honor women in horror. She also has a couple of short stories coming out later in 2013: "Paper and Pencil, Skin and Ink" will be appearing in *A Darke Phantastique*, edited by Jason Brock and "How to Save a Life" in Nightscape Press' *Best of Volume One*. You can find her on Facebook where she sometimes "likes" more than posts or on Twitter as @Chris_Marrs.